EMILY POSTS

EMILY POSTS

TANYA LLOYD KYI

tundra

Text copyright © 2024 by Tanya Lloyd Kyi
Jacket art copyright © 2024 by Ericka Lugo

Tundra Books, an imprint of Tundra Book Group,
a division of Penguin Random House of Canada Limited

All rights reserved. The use of any part of this publication reproduced, transmitted in any form or by any means, electronic, mechanical, photocopying, recording, or otherwise, or stored in a retrieval system, without the prior written consent of the publisher — or, in case of photocopying or other reprographic copying, a license from the Canadian Copyright Licensing Agency — is an infringement of the copyright law.

Publisher's note: This book is a work of fiction. Names, characters, places and incidents either are the product of the author's imagination or are used fictitiously, and any resemblance to actual persons living or dead, events, or locales is entirely coincidental.

Library and Archives Canada Cataloguing in Publication

Title: Emily Posts / Tanya Lloyd Kyi.
Names: Kyi, Tanya Lloyd, 1973- author.
Identifiers: Canadiana (print) 20220482985 | Canadiana (ebook) 20220483000 | ISBN 9781774882047 (hardcover) | ISBN 9781774882054 (EPUB)
Classification: LCC PS8571.Y52 E45 2024 | DDC jC813/.6—dc23

Published simultaneously in the United States of America by Tundra Books of Northern New York, an imprint of Tundra Book Group, a division of Penguin Random House of Canada Limited

Library of Congress Control Number: 2022951648

Edited by Lynne Missen
Jacket designed by Gigi Lau
The text was set in Minion Pro.

Printed in Canada

www.penguinrandomhouse.ca

1 2 3 4 5   28 27 26 25 24

For my family

1

Star Power

I love an attentive audience.

I take my seat at the head of the library table and tuck my hair behind one ear, so my hoop earrings are visible. (I'm trying to start a trend.) Then I smile encouragingly at my team.

They beam back at me. Well, Daniella does. On the other side of the table, Reza stares at his phone. Simone is late.

She whirls into the library a minute later, in a fabulous pleated skirt. And . . . she's wearing hoop earrings!

"Let the ruckus begin," she says, sliding in beside Reza.

"Thank you all for coming," I say, which is a more respectful way to start a meeting. Simone is my very best friend in the entire world and has excellent fashion sense, but Mr. Chadwick made the right choice when he put me in charge of the podcast.

"We have a lot to cover. I've already uploaded a template for our October show, so please have a look."

They obediently check their phones.

We're planning our second-ever episode of *Cedarview Speaks*. This is the first year our school has had a podcast instead of a boring newspaper. Mr. Chadwick, our sponsor teacher, calls us his beta-testing team. I'm the producer, which means I'm in charge of making schedules, assigning stories, and basically everything else. Simone's our main host, and Daniella's our audio engineer. Reza is at the meeting too, but he only covers sports so he doesn't really count. (Not that I would ever tell him that. I'm as polite to Reza as I am to the more useful members of my team.)

"We upload this episode in less than three weeks," I tell them. "That means one week to research, a week to record our stories, and just enough time for post-production."

The recording and post-production all happen in our tiny studio, tucked at the back of the library behind our worktable.

As the team reviews my schedule, Mr. Chadwick pokes his head around a bookshelf.

"Did you see the new mic?"

Our librarian is completely bald, which makes it especially obvious when his eyes sparkle. He sounds as if he bought us a puppy.

Daniella gives him a thumbs-up. She also blushes. Daniella has the classic pale skin of a redhead and she basically blushes as soon as anyone looks at her.

"Great choice, Mr. Chadwick," Simone says.

"Professional-quality condenser mic. Same thing they use at radio stations," he says. "I did my research."

Above him, the *CA Energy Supports Learning Everywhere!* banner flutters slightly in the draft from a heating vent.

Mr. Chadwick says that CA Energy is one of the biggest corporations in the whole country, and we're lucky they take an interest in local education. They're our biggest podcast sponsor. Well, they're our only sponsor.

"If I'd had all this equipment in high school, I'd be a broadcast journalist today. You'd be watching me on the news every night," Mr. Chadwick says.

This seems unlikely. Sometimes Mr. Chadwick's a little overly enthusiastic about the podcast. And there are only so many great things we can say about the new microphone, so we end up silently staring at him.

He shifts his gaze to me. "You good, Emily?"

"All good." I nod.

"Great. I need a coffee."

He disappears.

"Okay, let's continue," I say.

"Let's," Simone echoes. "I got such good feedback about our principal-for-a-day story in September. We'll probably have a ton of new listeners this month, so our episode needs to sizzle." She flashes jazz hands before opening her notebook.

One day, Simone's going to design sustainable fashion. She'll probably live in Paris. With her chic black bob and her makeup skills, she'll fit right in. But the jazz hands are a little much.

Besides, she's not the producer.

I lean forward. "Bina, that girl in sixth grade, swears she saw a rat in the cafeteria. A rat!"

"That's entirely gross." Simone shudders.

Daniella says something inaudible, as usual.

Reza rubs his hands together. "A little extra protein for the chili surprise."

Cedarview Cafeteria's mystery meat: No longer a mystery?

Mr. Chadwick says we can only promote our podcast within the school. But if we were allowed to boost it publicly, I could use that line as clickbait on YouHappy.

This past summer, I finally convinced my mom to let me get my own YouHappy account so I can prepare for my future career as an online influencer. Mom's only rule is that I'm not allowed to include photos of myself. Which is ridiculous. I'm trying — desperately — to change her mind. I'm also trying to attract new followers. I only have thirty, and three of those are bots with handles like @Texan5589567. As soon as I have more real followers, I'm definitely going to block the bots.

Reza's still talking about rats.

"Horriblific!" Simone shudders. "Okay, I'll follow up on that story."

"And what about profiles of some new students?" I suggest. "I think there's the guy who moved here from Spain, and that curly-haired girl from Ohio."

"I shall produce profiles of perfection." She scribbles diligently in her notebook.

"Reza, what's on your roster?"

"Practices start Monday. First game is next week."

He doesn't say what sport he's talking about, and I don't particularly care. I make a note to leave time for his piece.

"Daniella, you'll write our promo? Mr. Chadwick's going to put it on the school website."

Her lips move, but I don't hear her answer. Partly because she's incapable of volume and partly because just then Reza bangs the underside of the table with his knee.

I give him my best producer-like stare. "What are you doing?"

"Sorry," he mutters. "Taking my shoe off. Slipped."

Reza has long bangs that hang halfway over his brown eyes, and the most ridiculously long eyelashes. They're wasted on him.

I don't even bother asking why he's taking his shoe off. I turn to Simone instead. "We're going to record that sixth-grader's spoken word piece, right? Has she picked a title for it?"

"It's called 'Freedom from the Overlords,'" she says, snorting.

Daniella wrinkles her nose.

"Any other story ideas?" I skim one more time through the run-of-show on my phone screen. We'll have an introduction with teaser headlines, then our most attention-grabbing story (probably the rats) to hook our listeners. Less interesting stuff will go in the middle, then we'll outro with a plug for November's episode. "We could use a bit more content."

"I think there's a climate march at the end of the month," Reza says. For some reason, he's partially under the table, but . . . did he just suggest something useful?

"Great idea," I say, trying not to sound shocked. "I'll cover that." The story can go right after the rat infestation in our lineup.

"You should record your advice segment, Emily," Simone reminds me.

"I don't think anyone sent us questions after last month's episode." Our suggestion that everyone bring baking soda to school to make their lockers smell better was . . . messy.

"We could ask people in the hallway about their problems," Simone says. "I'm sure someone needs advice."

"Maybe I can make up the questions *and* the answers." I write another note to myself. "We should —"

Simone yelps, making all of us jump.

She fishes something from the back of her shirt, examines it, and then pushes it at Reza, who's laughing so hard he's practically sliding under the table.

"You . . . rodent!"

"I put —" Reza gasps. "My sock! She thought . . . rat . . ." He seems incapable of breathing.

"It's not funny, and I don't want to touch your stinky socks!"

Mr. Chadwick's face appears above the bookshelf. "What's going on over there?"

"He put his stinky sock down my back! I thought it was a rat!" Simone says.

Reza shrugs innocently.

"Aaaand, that's a wrap. We're done here." I nod to Mr. Chadwick and gather my things.

We adjourn the meeting and head off to chase rodents, fabricate advice, and cover the news of the world. Or, in this case, the happenings of Cedarview Middle School, population 545.

"We'd have more listeners — and more followers — if this school was bigger," I tell Simone as we leave the library.

She bumps my shoulder with hers. "Fortunately, you and I can bring the drama all by ourselves."

And I can hardly argue with that.

The next morning, Simone and I stand behind the podium on the gymnasium stage. We're wearing color-coordinated tops (mine turquoise and hers a complementary purple) and, of course, our silver hoops.

"Welcome to Cedarview Middle School and our Friday assembly," we say in unison. "Our names are Simone Ahn and Emily Laurence, and we'll be your MCs today. Please stand for our national anthem."

Sometimes, the assembly MCs mumble into their microphones and no one can understand what they're saying. But Simone and I are naturally attuned to one another. Cooperation is one of our most fabulous talents. Plus, we practiced on the phone last night.

Once everyone's settled back in their seats, we remind them of the Cedarview motto ("Be Kind, Be True, Be Fair") and announce that Division 3 will patrol the school grounds for litter. Then I introduce Mr. Lau, the principal, to make his usual speech.

When Simone and I sit down in the VIP chairs along the side of the stage, Ms. Truby, our social studies teacher, leans toward us. She's the one who organizes our assemblies.

"Well done, girls," she says. "I may have to cancel the usual rotation and use you every month."

I give her my best smile. I've been sitting through these assemblies for more than two years now, knowing the entire time that I could do a *much* better job of leading them. It's nice to have someone finally recognize my skills.

At the microphone, Mr. Lau clears his throat. "And now, I have other exciting news," he says.

Simone snorts, which is impolite but completely understandable. Mr. Lau's news is never exciting. It tends to be special "quiet time" because of International Silent Reading Week, or a new bulletin board to be installed in the main hallway. Principals don't have quite the same definition of "exciting news" as regular people do.

Then I hear the words "best-selling author," and my head pops up.

". . . various TV roles before launching her writing career. We are extremely fortunate to have this opportunity, presented by CoastFresh as part of their Future-Friendly Green Initiatives campaign."

Ooh . . . they should be our second podcast sponsor. I think the school already has some sort of sponsorship deal with CoastFresh, and the company provides a lot of our cafeteria food. Maybe they'd fund a story about —

"Who? Who's Mr. Lau talking about?" Simone whispers.

"I missed that part," I say.

Ms. Truby raises her eyebrows at us, forcing me to bring out my winning smile again. Emily Post, 1920s etiquette expert and my own personal idol, says: "To make a pleasant and friendly impression is not alone good manners, but equally good business." Or, in my case, equally good strategizing to get an A in social studies.

Mr. Lau starts a video on the drop-down screen behind him. When the CoastFresh logo fades, a smiling, waving woman with long, dark hair appears.

I gasp. "THAT'S ASHA JAMIL!"

A date flashes at the bottom of the screen.

"SHE'S COMING TO CEDARVIEW ON OCTOBER 28. WE CAN MEET HER!" Simone whisper-yells back, not even noticing Ms. Truby's reproving look.

Guess which TV star is making a surprise splashdown at our middle school!?!

I can't wait to post that on YouHappy at lunch hour.

Asha Jamil is not just any star. She played an astronaut and environmental scientist on a show called *Outer Orbit*. She's entirely responsible for my level of environmental knowledge. From space — even from fake space on a TV show — Earth looks so stunning that you automatically want to protect it.

Asha's character died in a tragic accident as her landing shuttle splashed into the Atlantic. After that, Asha started writing books as well as acting. She's been on the *New York Times* bestseller list practically forever.

According to the video, she's the spokesperson for the CoastFresh Future-Friendly Green Initiatives campaign — something about going green in the next fifty years — and she's touring schools to talk about her new kids' book.

"And hopefully about penthouse living and poodle owning," Simone whispers. "Asha has the MOST adorable poodle in the history of the universe."

Maybe I can get a poodle photo while she's here.

Meet my favorite astronaut's out-of-this-world pet.

"Thanks for listening. I can't wait to see you." Asha waves from the screen as the CoastFresh logo reappears. Everyone in the gym applauds.

"Emily, we have to seize this opportunity." Simone squeezes my arm.

"I know!" I squeeze her right back. My smile is practically trying to escape my face, and I can already imagine shaking hands with Asha. Since Mr. Lau often chooses *me* to give tours of our school to new students, I'm perfectly prepared to host guests. I can show Asha our eighth-grade social studies projects and our art pieces. And, of course, the podcasting studio. I'll introduce her to the teachers . . .

Reza's basketball friend, Bryce, has somehow stolen one of Reza's shoes. He sends it sailing over the heads of the rest of the eighth grade.

Mr. Lau stops the video and glares until the boys settle down. This gives me time to think of all the things I share with Asha. We're both concerned about animal extinctions. We're both polite human beings (unlike Bryce, who is trying to steal a second shoe). And we both understand the power of social media. She is an absolute star on YouHappy.

"Girls?" Mr. Lau is standing above us, eyebrows raised.

We scurry to the podium and introduce the birthday kids of the month.

I stumble through the names. All I can see in my head is an image of me talking to Asha as she smiles beatifically, impressed by my encyclopedic knowledge of her career.

My stomach bubbles and flutters at the idea. I have to take a deep breath.

"Focus!" I whisper to myself.

But now I'm picturing Asha once she's an old woman. She'll be introducing my TED Talk about modern-day etiquette and social influence.

Aging TV astronaut gives star treatment to universally loved influencer.

"I've known Emily Laurence since she was a student," she'll say. "Even then, her potential was obvious."

I absolutely *have* to meet her. It's practically my destiny.

2

Snacks Gone Wrong

When I open the front door of our townhouse after school, I find Richard sitting on the living room floor, his giant legs stretched across the hardwood. Mom leans against a stack of boxes with her feet propped in his lap.

"Hi, honey," she says.

"How goes it, Em?" Richard asks. He doesn't pause in his foot rubbing, which is really not something I should have to see.

"Fine, thank you," I say. "How's the unpacking?"

As far as I can tell, there are just as many boxes as there were this morning. One of my mom's inspirational posters leans haphazardly against the wall. It says: "Follow your dreams. They know the way." The words float above a spectacular rainbow. But somehow, I don't believe Mom is truly dreaming of getting these boxes unpacked.

"We're getting there," she says, as if reading my mind.

This is entirely unlike her. She hates to procrastinate.

She never sits on the floor. And she would never, ever agree to have her feet rubbed in public.

Then Richard whispers something in her ear and scoots closer so he can kiss her. *French* kiss her. RIGHT IN FRONT OF ME.

What is happening?

I avert my eyes and head for the kitchen.

My mom and dad were never really together. Well, I mean, obviously they were *together* at some point, but not for very long, and Mom says fatherhood wasn't "part of the picture" for him. He lives across the continent, and even though I've met him a few times when he's visited, he seems like a stranger. A polite stranger. With a large nose, which I thankfully didn't inherit.

Anyway, Mom and I always lived by ourselves, in an apartment across from Almond Park. Then, last year, she met Richard. They rented this townhouse together, we moved at the end of September, and they're getting married next summer. This should all have been done in reverse, if you ask me, but no one did.

I like Richard. His beard and his curly hair make him look like a friendly grizzly bear. But our move has come with a lot of . . . "adjustments," as Mom would say. One of those adjustments is licking an apple when I enter the kitchen.

His name is Ocean.

Does that make him sound wise and serene? He's not. He's a freckly, eight-year-old terror.

I find a place for my backpack between a half-empty box of cereal and Mom's favorite ceramic rooster, actually a cookie jar that cock-a-doodle-doos whenever someone opens the lid. (I bought it for her as a birthday present when I was nine, before I developed taste and discernment.) When I turn around, Ocean is still licking.

"What are you doing?"

"Practicing kissing," he says.

"MOM!"

I hear a box tip over and a few muffled swear words and giggles before Mom and Richard appear in the doorway.

"What?" Mom pants, scanning the kitchen.

I point to Ocean. "Ask him what he's doing."

"I'm practicing kissing," Ocean says, as if he's explaining his math homework or talking about dinosaurs, both of which would be rational things for an eight-year-old boy to be doing.

I can tell Mom is trying not to laugh.

Richard doesn't even try. "An apple," he says, bending his mouth to the crook of Mom's neck. "I should have thought of that. I could probably use more practice."

This is so inappropriate, I can't find words to protest.

"Sorry, Emily," Richard says. But he doesn't seem sorry at all.

I turn to my mom. She's the event organizer at one of the fanciest hotels in the city. She coordinates everything from conferences to bat mitzvahs. The biggest events are usually weddings, and she has to know all the social rules, so she can seat the mother-of-the-bride in the right place and ensure the forks are in order. She's serious about politeness and proper etiquette. Of all people, Mom should recognize that this situation is completely unacceptable.

But before she can say anything, Ocean takes a gigantic bite of his apple with the loudest crunch ever. Richard cracks up. Mom joins in. Then Ocean joins in, even though he probably has no idea what they're laughing about.

Years from now, this story will be a top thread on my YouHappy feed.

How I was psychologically scarred by my mother's new relationship.

For now, I give up and leave the room. Not one of these people has any appreciation for proper behavioral standards. Not even my mother!

Also, I may never eat an apple again.

Once I'm shut safely in my room, I grab my phone. I limit myself to reading three of Asha Jamil's latest posts. Then I start researching my podcast stories.

With a few clicks, I find the event listing for the climate march. It's on Friday, October 29. (The day after Asha Jamil's visit!) There's lots of information, so I write the script for Simone to read as she introduces the segment. Then I stare at my phone for a while. Simone sent me the contact number for the march organizer, Mya. Apparently, she runs the Climateers club at the high school just down the block from Cedarview.

I should really phone Mya and record a few quotes. But she's a twelfth-grader and I don't want my questions to sound middle-school-ish. I need *serious* questions.

A notification dings.

New Video: The Palette Pixie

I absolutely LOVE every single post by The Palette Pixie. She created a whole social media empire by giving makeup tips, and now she talks about ways other girls can build online influence.

I'm dying to watch her new video. And I'm quite positive that phoning Mya is not a productive use of time at this exact moment.

I send Mya a quick text instead.

> Hi! This is Emily Laurence. I'm creating a podcast piece for Cedarview Middle School. Can you leave me a voice mail with a quote or two about the climate march, please?

There. That sounds professional. And while a phone message won't have the ideal recording quality for our podcast, I'm sure Daniella can make it work.

I wait a few minutes, hoping my phone will immediately ring, but there's nothing. If I add a few vague sentences to Simone's script, the lack of an interview might not be obvious. She can say "Organizers are hoping . . ." and I'll invent something. Something plausible, of course.

This plan leaves me free to watch the newest Palette Pixie instalment.

I'm about to press play when Mom swings open my bedroom door.

"You're not looking at inappropriate pictures, are you?" she says.

"Mom!"

"Who knows?" Mom says. "I hear it's a serious issue with kids on the internet."

"MOM!"

She blinks innocently.

"I'm writing a script."

She plops onto the bed beside me. "How was school?"

"School was fine. But I came home to find we're living with Neanderthals."

She smiles as if I'm joking. "They'll take some getting used to."

"Mom." I drop my voice to a whisper. "Ocean left the bathroom *so* stinky this morning. I had to —"

"Well, he can't help that," she says, her smile fading. "And it's hardly a polite topic."

Ocean's footsteps thunder down the stairs, then back up again.

"I can't find it ANYWHERE!" he hollers.

Mom sighs. "I should help."

Ocean's inability to act like a normal human being is probably another impolite topic. I'm sure he's looking for a torn-up comic book or a model poo he made with clay, and I don't think Mom needs to solve every fake emergency.

"Mom, do you think he needs . . . treatment?"

"Ocean?"

I nod, and I don't appreciate it when she laughs at me.

"Oh, Emily. We're just not accustomed to sharing our space. He's a perfectly average eight-year-old boy. And we'll get used to him."

This seems doubtful. But at least Mom and I will have plenty of quiet time together on Sunday. The hotel where she works is called The Allegra. Every Sunday morning, we order fancy drinks from their downstairs café, then Mom catches up on an hour or two of work while I finish my homework. It's been our mother-daughter tradition for years.

"We can talk more at the hotel," I say as she heads for the hall.

I got a little emotional the week before we moved. The couch and TV were the only things left in our old living room. Mom and I were curled up, ignoring the rest of the packing we had to do. We found a pretty good movie on Netflix. But at one point, as the mom on screen sat on the couch with her new boyfriend, I burst into tears.

So embarrassing. I'm usually much more mature.

Anyway, that night Mom promised our hotel dates would continue, and some things would stay exactly the same as always.

But now, as she turns back from the doorway, I can tell by the look on her face . . .

There are no decaf caramel lattes on the menu this weekend.

"I'm so sorry," she says. "I meant to mention it earlier. Richard and I need to meet with the property manager about repairs, and he could only see us on Sunday morning."

Somehow, despite feeling as if I've been impaled by a stir stick, I manage to shrug.

"That's fine."

She comes back to sit on the edge of my bed.

"I really do want to continue our dates. I'll make it up to you next week."

Another shrug.

After a minute of uncomfortable silence, Mom leans over and gives me a sideways hug. Then she picks up my phone from the bed and checks out my screen. Giving Mom my security code was one of the requirements for having my own phone.

"What's your script about?" she asks.

Apparently, she's never heard of privacy. Also, she is a master of subject changing.

"Oh, the climate march!" she says.

"It's a piece for the October podcast," I tell her reluctantly.

"It needs a little pizzazz," she says, after READING THE WHOLE THING WITHOUT PERMISSION. "Are you going to record some quotes?"

I fume silently. Everyone's an editor. And she has no idea how stinky Ocean left the bathroom. Also, I can't believe she moved directly from canceling our mother-daughter time to criticizing my script.

"IT'S GONE. IT'S GONE," Ocean shouts. More frantic running.

Mom gives my shoulders one last squeeze and heads for the hall to deal with the situation.

"It can't be gone," she tells Ocean.

"Susan, my gum is GONE," he insists. "And I had half a package left!"

"It must be here somewhere. Let's check your backpack."

Gum. That's his emergency. I get up, swing my bedroom door closed, then flop into my desk chair. There's a burning feeling beneath my ribs. I grit my teeth and take deep breaths, waiting for it to go away, but it's surprisingly stubborn.

Who needs a stupid latte? Ocean obviously requires constant entertainment and supervision, but I don't. I'm too old for weekly mom-and-daughter bonding. I was mostly setting aside Sunday mornings for Mom's sake, to help her adapt to all the changes in her life. But now I'll have extra time for my own projects. Developing my career as an influencer, for example. And also saving the world from climate change, which is something that deserves basically all my time and energy. And top-quality voice recordings, too.

Just to prove my own independence, professionalism, and lack of need for a mother, I sit myself down at my desk. I grab my phone, get my recording app ready, and dial Mya's number. She answers right away.

"Hello?"

"Hi. I'm Emily. I'm recording this call because I'm doing a piece for —"

"Oh, you're the podcaster! I got your text. Sorry I didn't call right away, I'm sooooo busy this week. The climate march has taken over my life. We're having Indigenous leaders open it from a stage in front of City Hall, and then someone from city council has agreed to speak, and I need about a hundred volunteers along the route. You don't want to help out, do you?"

"Well, I —"

"Oh, you know what would be amaZING? Could you put up posters in your school?" she asks.

"Sure?"

"Fabulous! And think about volunteering. I need first aid attendants, too. Do you have any certifications?"

"No, I —"

"You have nooooo idea how much work goes into something like this. It's bananas."

"How many —"

"I'm really, really hoping at least a thousand people will come. For a city the size of ours, that would be unbelievable. But I think we can do it. All the members of our Climateers club are promoting the event."

I barely get a couple more questions in before she abruptly stops.

"Oh, I have to go. Other line. Did you get what you needed?"

"Yes, I —"

"Great! Hope to see you there!"

And she's gone.

Mya is a born influencer. If I'd had a few more minutes, I would have told her about The Palette Pixie, and she could have found tips to triple her reach.

I replay the whole interview, trying to isolate quotes to use in my piece. It takes me a few tries because Mya talks so quickly. In the end, though, I choose a couple of good options. I include a few lines about the march as a youth-led initiative and a way that young people can show our commitment to the environment. And I even add something about taking the bus downtown that afternoon.

I don't specifically say that everyone should skip school, of course, but who will want to be in class when something like this is going on?

When I'm done, I set my phone down on my desk and glance contentedly around my room/professional office space. From the wall above my bookshelf, Emily Post gazes down at me, her long pearl necklace draped around an elegant neck. This poster hung in my room in our old apartment, too. At the bottom, in an elegant cursive scroll, the words read: "Because a house is little is no reason that it can not be as perfect in every detail — perhaps more so — as the palace of the multiest millionaire."

Even if the rest of the townhouse is a lost cause, I plan to make every detail perfect within my room. And that feeling beneath my ribs when I was talking to Mom? That was probably heartburn. Richard packed a chicken wrap for my lunch and it was ridiculously spicy.

3

Personal Space

Principal Lau calls my name as I walk past the school office on Monday morning. He's wearing a red tie and a blue button-down shirt, the same thing he wore at the assembly on Friday. The buttons of his shirt strain a little across his belly.

"I'm so glad I caught you," he says. He gestures to a tall girl standing beside him. She has a butter-yellow scarf tied around her neck in a way that should make her seem forty years old but somehow looks absolutely perfect.

"You two are going to have a lot in common," Mr. Lau says. "Even your names are similar. Emily, this is Amelie."

"With an *A*," she clarifies. "The French way."

My smile wavers. The new girl has the type of long, strawberry blond hair I've always wanted. The color that could never, ever be called "dirty blond" the way mine is. And she has giant green eyes that look as if they popped off a manga cat. Suddenly, I intensely wish my name were

Amelie instead of Emily. Even though Emily Post is a great role model who knew how to use good manners and write proper thank-you notes, her name's not nearly as poetic as Amelie.

"Amelie's our newest eighth-grader. She just transferred. Can you give her a quick tour before you head to class?" Mr. Lau asks.

"Of course." I paste on my most polite smile. I suppose I'll gain extra practice as a tour guide. (Soon-to-be tour guide for Asha Jamil! That thought makes me feel immeasurably better.)

Just as Amelie is about to say something, Marcus races past us and ducks around a corner of the hallway.

Marcus is in sixth grade. We went to the same elementary school, and I was his Big Buddy when he was in kindergarten. I've had a soft spot for him ever since. He's super smart, he loves to talk about outer space, and he's always polite . . . if you don't mind that he sometimes sprints away in the middle of a conversation.

"Where was that kid going?" Amelie asks.

Marcus's aide appears, lumbering after him.

"Stop right there, buddy," he yells.

His words seem to startle our principal into action. Mr. Lau joins the chase.

"Does this happen often?" Amelie asks, once they've disappeared around the corner.

I shrug. "Marcus isn't a fan of classrooms. Last week, he disappeared for a whole day and the rest of us got free periods because the teachers had to search for him. They finally found him behind the kiln in the art room."

I grin at her before I remember my responsibilities. Quickly, I show her the bathrooms, the art room, and the science lab. I introduce her to Mr. Chadwick in the library.

"Nice to meet you, Amelie," he says. "Oh, you should have Emily show you the new microphone while you're here. State of the art!"

He's getting a bit ridiculous about this microphone, and tech equipment is not a normal school tour stop. But Amelie loves our podcasting space.

"It's so adorable, all tucked away here!"

"It used to be a storage space." I'm not sure an old book room can be adorable, but it *is* impressive. There are three spinning office chairs, and a long desk with our computer monitor, our mixer, and — of course — the new microphone.

"And you produce the podcast every month? How many of you?"

"Four. We're the beta testers. Next year, Mr. Chadwick is going to run an entire podcasting club."

"Amazing! Let me know if you need help," she says.

"Sure," I say. But obviously, as producer, I have the podcast completely under control. I can't imagine I'll need help.

I lead Amelie to the cafeteria in the basement, stopping at the table where Simone and I eat every day. Then I point out the nut-free table, and also the table-of-perpetual-stickiness where the boys hold juice-box battles.

"It's sort of dangerous to cross the aisle here. But at least they're eco-friendly juice-box battles. My best friend Simone and I started a recycling program for the school last year. Organizing is one of our most fabulous talents."

I hope that sounds like useful information and not like bragging.

By the time the bell rings, we're on our way upstairs toward the eighth-grade homerooms. The hallways are crowded now, and we're jostled by elbows and backpacks. When we're halfway up the stairwell, Reza and Bryce slide down the banister, against traffic, yelling "Steee-rike!" as if they're human bowling balls. A few steps above us, Daniella loses her balance and almost goes flying. Amelie and I press ourselves against the wall.

If someone filmed this whole scene in slow motion, it would instantly go viral on YouHappy.

As soon as I can move again, I turn toward Amelie, intending to apologize on behalf of humanity. But she's grinning.

"This is exactly what I wanted." She turns her bright green eyes on me. "I transferred from Lake Pointe West because I needed to experience the true public school atmosphere. And you have everything: arts initiatives, a diverse student population, lots of energy. There's so much we can do with this place."

What's that supposed to mean? We're not a social experiment. And Lake Pointe West is a ridiculously expensive private school near the university. Maybe it's not on purpose, but Amelie makes Cedarview sound like it's in need of a makeover.

It might be time to drop her at her classroom.

"What homeroom are you?"

"Division twelve."

I've probably misheard her. "What teacher?"

She glances at her paper. "Ms. Flores's eighth-grade homeroom."

Which is *my* homeroom. What kind of misguided school puts two people with almost the same name in the same homeroom?

I'm still processing this news when Simone appears. I make proper introductions as we enter our class. Then, barely three minutes later, Ms. Flores says the words I expected to hear only in my nightmares.

"Amelie and Emily. That's so sweet! Maybe we'll call you Amelie C. and Emily L., so we don't get confused."

She smiles as if she's said something clever.

"Please welcome Amelie C. to Cedarview," she tells the class. "I know you'll help her feel right at home."

Just like that, I'm someone who needs an extra letter for identification. I do *not* feel right at home with Amelie in my class.

🎙

I head to the library at lunchtime because Mr. Chadwick never manages to download the audio files properly and he always wants a written list of what we're planning.

The library's open, but I can't find him. "Mr. Chadwick?"

It's a bit of a maze in here. There's the checkout desk along the back wall, with a giant fish tank beside it to divide the space. On the left of the tank are worktables, the podcasting studio, and the non-fiction bookshelves. On the opposite side of the tank there's a cozy reading nook with yellow and blue beanbag chairs and a plush blue recliner, surrounded by book racks. And all the other space is filled with more shelves. As I peek between them, looking for our missing librarian, Simone appears beside me.

"I thought I'd find you here," she says. "What do you think of our newest arrival? Did you hear that her name is French? Do you think she's been to Paris?"

Before I can respond, she gasps. "What if she's met Caroline Reboux?"

Caroline is Simone's very favorite designer, famous for her elaborate hats.

"Isn't she dead?"

"Well, yes, but maybe there's a monument to her in France or something."

"You want to ask Amelie if she's seen a statue?" It's possible my friend has lost her mind.

"Yes. So, can we hang out with her?" Simone's bob bounces.

"With Caroline?" I say hopefully.

"With Amelie!"

I sigh. "Sure."

I'm not exactly longing to make friends with Amelie, but I've had a few hours to decide how to handle her. I've chosen a strategy of reserved politeness. I'm quite sure that's what Emily Post would recommend. She wrote that people who are extremely in demand in society have to be careful about being too friendly, or they might be besieged by new people. Besieged! So . . . reserved politeness.

"It's super exciting to have someone new in our class," Simone says.

She and I have been best friends since the first day of fourth grade, when we wore matching polka-dot tights.

It's been obvious ever since that we share the same great taste, and Simone has been the perfect practice audience for my influencing. Though, at this moment, I think I should influence her expectations.

"I think this new girl might be a bit strange," I say.

I stop to use the fish tank as a mirror, adjusting the front of my hair so it covers a pimple on my forehead. One never knows when someone will be snapping pictures. As a social media star, it will be important not to have awkward middle school photos floating around the internet.

Persephone, the largest of the goldfish, makes bubble *O*s of agreement from the other side of the glass.

Simone appears in the reflection behind me, wrinkling her button nose. "Strange how?"

"Well, she . . ." I rack my brain to think of a specific example. "She said she was here for the true public school experience, as if we were a social experiment."

Simone looks confused.

"It was the way she said it." I repeat Amelie's words in a snotty voice, adding a hair toss.

"And did she flick her hair like that?"

"It was implied."

Simone gasps. "I can't believe she did that. It's entirely offensive."

"She didn't look appropriately horrified when I told her about the juice-box battles, either."

"Those are abominable!" Simone wrinkles her nose. "I wish Mr. Lau would ban juice boxes. Last week my blue sweater got completely splooshed. You remember, right? My favorite one? It's ruined."

Simone has the wardrobe of a model, and it's nearly impossible to keep track of her sweaters. Also, we're getting off topic. But before I can think of more reasons Amelie's going to be a problem, we hear a noise from the reading nook on the other side of the tank.

Simone and I lock eyes.

Spy steals shocking middle school secrets.

Someone's been hiding back there while we've discussed serious, confidential issues. My stomach clenches.

"Hello?" Simone calls, peeking past the fish tank.

A rustle.

We investigate. On the other side of the bookshelves, in the depths of the blue reading chair and mostly covered by throw cushions, sits . . .

"It's only Marcus," Simone says.

What a relief. And now that I see him, I remember Mr. Lau and the aide running down the hallway this morning.

"Having a rough day?" I ask him.

He nods.

The bell rings to signal the end of lunch, but I feel bad leaving him here.

"Anything we can do to help?" I ask.

He stares at the floor.

"Rob's an evil space robot," he says finally.

Rob is Marcus's aide.

"Teachers and aides." Simone sighs. "They're all annoying. It's practically in their job descriptions. Do you know I was talking to Mr. Gill once, and he called fashion a distraction? A distraction! He —"

"Rob's probably not completely evil," I interrupt. "He must have redeeming qualities."

Marcus holds up his hands, as if they're scales. "Is he an evil space robot? Is he not an evil space robot?"

"Marcus, do you think one of us should go to the office? And then maybe the school can call your mom?" I ask. I've seen Marcus's mom here a lot. I think she comes to collect him every time he causes trouble for the teachers.

Eventually, he nods. "That would be a reasonable course of action."

Simone heads for the door to get help.

As I cast around for something to talk about, my eyes land on one of the book displays. Front and center is Asha Jamil's new book, *How to Save the Planet*. I grab it from the shelf for Marcus.

"Have you read this one? She's an astronaut. Well, she played one on TV."

He looks mildly interested.

"She still loves everything about space and science and the environment. You're into space, right?" We made a model of the solar system when I was his Big Buddy.

He nods, reaching for the book.

"It's mostly about how we should treat the Earth. She writes about what she learned while pretending to be in orbit."

"Pretending to be in orbit?"

"I guess she had lots of time to think, floating around on her TV set. She's visiting our school, you know."

Marcus looks as if he's going to ask more questions, but Simone arrives just then with a whole troop in tow: Mr. Lau, Mr. Chadwick, and Rob.

"What are we going to do with you, Marcus?" Rob asks.

"Expulsion?" Marcus sounds hopeful.

Mr. Lau sighs.

Mr. Chadwick seems to be biting back a smile. "Would you like to check out that book before you go?"

Marcus looks at *How to Save the Planet* in his hands, then points to me.

"Emily recommended it."

"Then I'm sure it's excellent." Mr. Chadwick is definitely smiling now.

But the pointing must have reminded Mr. Lau that Simone and I are standing there. He sends us straight to class.

When we get to social studies, Ms. Truby says, "Good of you to finally join us, Simone and Emily."

I don't appreciate her sarcasm. But at least she doesn't call me Emily L.

4

Epic Etiquette Fails

When I get home from school, the packing boxes have been rearranged. There's a tall, wide stack of them near the front door. Richard crouches behind the tower.

"Emily, get down!" he whispers urgently.

Before I understand what's happening, a beanbag sails though the air and smacks me directly between my eyes.

"Ouch!"

I rub my forehead. Ocean peeks from behind another stack of boxes, looking only slightly guilty.

"Are you okay?" Richard asks. "We found Ocean's beanbags this afternoon. Usually he uses them for juggling, but the boxes make great forts, and . . ."

Should beanbags be classified as weapons? Now that I've been maimed in a beanbag battle, I say yes.

If I were allowed to post pictures of myself, I could add a selfie of what's probably a huge red mark on my forehead.

I stare at Richard.

"Your mom called. She's working late," he says.

Mother abandons her child in a war zone.

"Will you excuse me, please? I have homework."

Once I've crossed enemy lines, climbed the stairs, and reached the refuge of my own room, I pull my notebook from my backpack. I have an idea for my future house. It will not be filled with box forts. It's going to have clean white walls. A bank of glass display cabinets for my favorite books. An office with a functional but stylish chair (one that spins). And, preferably, a secret library with an entrance no one but me will be able to find. I've just decided that it can be hidden behind a chest of drawers. A bookcase would be too obvious.

There's a tap on my not-so-secret door. I close my journal as Richard tentatively pokes his head into the room. He's carrying a peace offering of cinnamon toast.

"Sorry about all that," he says, holding out the plate.

I stare at it, considering. I *could* throw his toast in the trash. It would make a highly dramatic chapter in my future autobiography. On the other hand, Emily Post would disapprove. And I hate to miss good cinnamon toast.

"I made it specially," he says.

Because of Richard's beard, only the tops of his cheeks turn pink when he blushes.

I reach for the toast.

"I know this is a big transition for you," he says. "I sent Ocean to play with Jackson, so you could have some quiet time to do your homework."

Along with its more desirable points (only six blocks from my school, and a small front yard with a flower garden), this new townhouse came with an eight-year-old boy next door. Because every neighborhood has downsides.

"It's okay. I can probably survive a beanbag attack," I say grudgingly.

He looks relieved. "Ocean has a lot of energy, and he's still adjusting to his mom moving away."

Ocean's mom took a job in Los Angeles, so he won't be staying with her until the Christmas holidays. Unfortunately for me.

"I know living with us isn't easy. But I really love you and Susan... um... your mom. And I'm so happy we were able to find this place together."

It's not easy to stay annoyed with Richard. And the toast is just as good as I expected.

"Your room looks great," he says, while I'm chewing.

Our new townhouse is kind of upside down. There's a main floor with the kitchen and living room. The big bedroom and bathroom for Mom and Richard are way down in the basement — or "the garden level," as the rental ad described it. And Ocean and I have our bedrooms upstairs, where we share a bathroom.

Because I'm the oldest, Richard and Mom gave me first choice between the upstairs rooms. For obvious reasons, I picked the one with the ultra-YouHappy-able bay window. I've placed my desk right in front of it. The purple duvet on my bed is from our apartment, but Mom bought me a new rug to match. And I have a tall bookshelf, where I've arranged my favorite titles alphabetically by author.

Richard glances through the spines.

"This is a lot of books. Are you going to be a writer?"

"Sort of . . . but in short sentences."

After a crumb flies from my mouth, I make myself stop and chew. Richard waits patiently.

"I'm going to be an influencer," I say, finally.

His bushy eyebrows knit together. "What does that mean?"

"It's sharing fashion or decorating tips or cooking ideas on social media. Then, once you build up a ton of followers, you set trends."

I can do all sorts of good for the world when I'm famous. For example, I'll promote recycling initiatives and recommend against wearing berets (they really don't flatter most people).

"This is a job?"

"Companies pay you to promote their brands."

Shockingly, Richard is still listening. He's even nodding a little.

I sit up straighter. If I can convince Richard that I need to start my influencing career now, he might be able to persuade my mom to let me post pictures of myself. Why didn't I think of this earlier? Now I have two parents . . . sort of. So, when one says no, I can ask the other one. I never before understood the advantages of two-parent families.

"Even micro-influencers, people with maybe twenty thousand followers, can earn hundreds of dollars per post."

"That's incredible," Richard says. Which proves that Mom has at least a modicum of taste in men.

"Once I have more followers on YouHappy, I can start contributing to our household finances."

Maybe that was too big a step. Richard has turned his attention back to my bookshelf. But I can convince him slowly, over the next few weeks.

He picks up a copy of Mom's all-time favorite book. My mom's the definition of an Emily Post super-fan — thus my name. And my twelfth birthday present was a 1920s edition of *Emily Post's Etiquette*, which would be worth a lot of money except that she found it tattered at a garage sale, with a coffee stain on its cover and its first ten pages ripped out.

I know the book is ridiculously old-fashioned, but I still love reading it. It's like an old movie — all the action happens at soirées and tea parties.

Richard runs a finger across the other books on my shelf. There are etiquette guides from different decades by people like Elsa Maxwell, and some biographies of advice columnists like Amy Vanderbilt and Princess Mysteria.

"Mom likes those books because she says manners are the foundation of good relationships, and we're losing the ability to relate to one another. But I think those women were influencers, like I want to be."

"Really?"

"They wrote newspaper columns and gave people advice on real-world problems. Emily Post even had a radio show. It's kind of like today, except now if we want to know how to wear ankle boots or what hairstyle is best for a job interview, we check social media accounts."

"I always wonder how to wear ankle boots."

I politely refrain from rolling my eyes.

Once Richard finishes flipping through *Etiquette*, he puts it carefully back on the shelf.

"You've gotten a lot done in here," he says, looking around.

"Well, you're supposed to unpack the boxes, not use them for defense. And not recline in the midst of them and . . . you know."

"Is that right?" His cheeks turn pink again.

I nod firmly.

He leaves the room while running his fingers through his beard. He's probably thinking deeply about my wisdom.

Once he's gone, I find myself staring again at my poster. I'm not sure whether Emily Post would have approved of us moving in with Richard and Ocean. The whole situation would have been scandalous in the 1920s.

On the other hand, Emily experienced some scandals of her own. She was married to a stockbroker name Edwin Post. They had a fancy house in a posh part of New York. But Edwin kept cheating on her with dancers and actresses. Then, a journalist tried to blackmail Edwin. The journalist said that unless Edwin paid him lots of money, he would publish pictures of Edwin with his latest girlfriend. Emily and the rest of the world would find out about his cheating!

Edwin had to decide . . . should he pay the journalist? Or should he confess to his wife?

He refused to pay. He confessed everything to Emily. People still found out about his affair with the actress, though. It was all horribly embarrassing for Emily, and she divorced him in 1905.

At that point, she was already a writer. But her career really took off once she was single. Her first etiquette book came out in 1922.

Anyway, I think Emily might have understood that not all families are exactly the same. And maybe she'd even understand why Mom fell in love with Richard and why we all moved in together. But I'm positively positive she would have recommended more time between those two things.

5

Vegan Manga Eyes

I drop onto my usual bench on Wednesday and pull out my lunch. Our cafeteria has been swathed in blue-and-yellow banners ever since CoastFresh foods appeared on the menu last year. So when Simone sits down across from me wearing a yellow scarf exactly like the one Amelie wore on Monday, it's a bit blinding. Especially when combined with the blue cafeteria tray and the yellow-striped wrapping of her CoastFresh cheeseburger.

Before I can complain about my retinas, Daniella appears.

"Can I sit with you?" she whispers.

I slide over to make room.

"Is it extra loud in here today?" She's barely audible above the noise of people calling to one another.

"Definitely." It doesn't help that, across the aisle, Reza and Bryce seem to be competing to see who can gargle the most chocolate milk for the longest amount of time.

I shake my head and dig my thermos from my lunch bag. When I take off the lid, Simone leans across the table.

"What's that amazing smell?"

Until this year, I made my own sandwiches, or sometimes Mom gave me money to buy cafeteria meals. Now Richard makes my lunches, and they're usually delicious. Richard teaches at a culinary school in the mornings, but his afternoons are flexible, which gives him plenty of time to cook for us.

"Richard says it's Indonesian." I show her the mixture of noodles, curried chicken bites, and green onions — leftovers from last night's dinner.

"Can I try a bite? One teensy bite?"

When I pass my noodles across the table, she rolls some onto her fork.

"This is absolutely divine," she says. "It's amazing what a true chef can do. Maybe he can give workshops here, for our cafeteria staff."

Ms. Lydia, the cafeteria supervisor and possibly the scariest person in the whole school, materializes between our table and the boys' table, where Reza and Bryce are now covered in streaks of chocolate. She points an accusing finger at them.

"Stop that! Now!"

I hold my breath until she walks away, back to her post in the corner. Beside me, I feel Daniella give a matching exhale.

Daniella's lunch is a jam sandwich cut in perfect squares, which she's eating in tiny, tiny bites. She pauses to say something, but I can't hear her.

I'm not sure Daniella and I would hang out if Mr. Chadwick hadn't put us on the podcast team together, but she doesn't seem to have a lot of other friends. She doesn't belong to any groups, if you don't count the computer club. Her habit of whispering is a little annoying. And at this moment, she looks extra stressed.

"Is everything okay?"

She tugs at a piece of her already ruffled hair. "Um . . . it's just that . . ."

Her voice disappears again.

"Take your time," I say, not because I want to but because it's what Emily Post would say.

"Bryce is copying off me," Daniella blurts. "It happened all last year, and now it's starting again. He sits beside me in every class."

Well, this seems like the sort of problem that needs an etiquette and advice specialist.

"Can you move your arm to hide your paper?" I ask.

"If I do, he makes things . . . uncomfortable."

It probably doesn't take much to make Daniella uncomfortable.

"And he calls me Soup Girl because my last name is Campbell, and he thinks that's funny. He says I turn red like tomato soup whenever he talks to me."

This is the longest whispered speech I've ever heard Soup Girl make. (It is a *little* funny.)

"Can't you tell one of your teachers?" Simone says.

She leans across the table to hear Daniella, and I manage to reclaim my thermos while she's distracted.

"Bryce will know I told on him. I don't mind helping, but —" She bites her lip.

"Daniella," I say firmly, "this isn't helping. What Bryce is doing is cheating. You're stressed out, and he isn't learning anything."

She nods uncertainly.

"You have two choices. You can sit down with Bryce at lunchtime and chat about the situation. Tell him you're unhappy."

Her eyes widen as she glances toward the juice-box table. "He won't —"

"Sometimes, a good heart-to-heart can work wonders," Simone says.

"I can't —"

"Or, you can stay after school and explain the problem to a teacher," I say.

"What if —"

"If you're worried about talking clear-ifically, you could try writing a letter instead," Simone suggests.

"To express yourself clearly," I say, in case Daniella still doesn't speak Simone-ese the way I do.

I'm about to offer some wording suggestions when Simone flashes her phone screen in our direction.

"Hey, Asha Jamil is going to the Meta Forward Banking National Media Awards. And LOOK at the incredibleness she gets to wear. She's chosen sustainable fashion. I'm in complete and utter awe."

Simone's had her own YouHappy account since sixth grade *and* she's allowed to post photos of herself, so she has more than two hundred followers. If I'd had an account for that long, I'd have thousands by now, but Simone doesn't have quite the same mastery of social media. Probably because she's not properly focused.

I lose track of Daniella's anxiety issues as I flip through the photos of Asha's dress. It really is stunning.

Suddenly, Simone waves her arms in the air. I look up to see Amelie walking into the cafeteria, her perfect hair glowing under the fluorescent lights. It's as if she's following me everywhere, to all the same classes. For the last couple of days she had to do math catch-up sessions at lunch, so I at least got a break. Today, no such luck.

"Why don't you eat with us?" Simone calls. "Sit right here, *ma chérie*. We'll give you the scoop on Cedarview secrets."

I *want* to say no, there's a limit of only one Emily/Amelie per table, and we're trying to have serious conversations here, about things like bullying and homework copying. But that wouldn't be polite. I manage to smile instead. Daniella has gone silent again.

"Are there many of these secrets?" The corner of Amelie's mouth quirks up, and a tiny dimple shows in her cheek.

Of course she has a dimple. I've always wanted one.

Simone smiles. "So many. *Beaucoup de* secrets."

Since when does Simone speak French? I give her a pointed look, which she ignores.

"For example," she says, leaning close to Amelie, "I'm almost entirely convinced that Mr. Chadwick has a crush on Ms. Flores."

I can't help gasping right along with Amelie. Even Daniella makes a slight squeak.

Simone nods. "This morning, she gave me a folder to carry to his classroom, and when he took the folder, he ran his fingers across the top of it. *Très romantique!*"

I'm not convinced by Simone's evidence, but this *is* an interesting theory.

"Hey, great scarf!" Amelie tells Simone.

"I knotted it exactly like you said," Simone says.

When did they have time to discuss the intricacies of scarf wearing?

"A minute ago, we were talking about Asha Jamil's visit," I tell Amelie. "You missed the assembly . . . did you hear the news that she's coming to Cedarview at the end of October? Two weeks and one day from now."

"I saw it on her tour schedule. I'm a huge fan," Amelie says.

Simone squeals. "That's *incroyable!*"

I can't tell which one of us she's talking to.

"Right," I say.

"Right? What about serendipitous?" Simone says. "What about *exceptionnel*? What about possibly world-changing, once the three of us put our heads together and decide how to welcome her?"

"Four of us," I amend, with a glance at Daniella. Not that she's going to be much use, but it's only proper to include her.

"Did you notice Asha's link to the anti-poverty group?" Amelie asks. "I already begged my parents to donate. I reposted her a bunch of times . . ."

Great. Amelie's probably another person who has way more followers than I do.

Whatever she says next is drowned out by a particularly loud crash from the juice-box-battle arena.

"It super loud in here," Amelie says. "And . . . strange."

She glances from the juice-dampened boys toward Marcus. He and his friends seem to be building a rocket ship with CoastFresh plastic forks.

But Amelie doesn't even know these people.

"I guess this is part of having a diverse school population," she says.

"We're not di —" I stop. Because we *are* diverse, but the way Amelie says it makes it sound as if we're on display at a zoo.

Then Ms. Lydia stomps over to accuse the juice-box boys of being gorillas, which means maybe we really are a zoo, and I'm too confused to say anything.

Simone can't comment. She's busy staring at Amelie's lunch. I wrap an arm protectively around what's left of my own food.

Amelie has pasta salad with cherry tomatoes, cucumbers, and olives.

"Do you want a bite?" she asks Simone, who nods eagerly.

"Fabulous," Simone says, when she's finished chewing. "It's like Greek salad with noodles instead of cheese."

"I can't eat cheese. I'm vegan," Amelie says.

Daniella's lips move.

"*Incroyable!*" Simone says, though a little flicker in her eyes makes me think she doesn't know what vegan means.

"My whole family believes strongly in animal rights," Amelie says.

"Interesting," I say. I have to, because Simone's mouth is full.

Daniella stares as if Amelie's a particularly fascinating

section of computer code. "There are terrible problems with meat in our diet," she whispers.

"You wouldn't believe the problems with meat in our diet," Amelie says.

I can't tell if she heard Daniella or not.

"Right," I say, looking back and forth between them and trying to seem knowledgeable.

"I'm sure you've heard that we keep chickens in cages so small their chests are permanently scarred," Amelie says. "And we pull the beaks off baby chickens so they can't peck each other to death."

Unfortunately, I have a big bite of Indonesian chicken curry in my mouth at the exact moment she says "beaks." Swallowing doesn't go well.

"That's disgusting!" Simone says, while I'm busy choking. "Oooh . . . you should start a vegan club. And create vegan lunch menus."

"Do you think people would be interested?" Amelie asks.

"Of course! Emily, you'd be interested, right?"

I manage a string of coughs.

"People will definitely want to learn about veganatarianism," Simone says.

"Veganism," Daniella whispers.

Seriously, I could die by asphyxiation and none of these people would notice.

Girl collapses in fatal choking incident. Friends overcome with guilt and regret.

"People already know a lot about those things," I say, once I finally manage to breathe. "For example, I'm perfectly aware that vegan food —"

"I'm a vegan too," Daniella whispers.

I turn to stare at her. "You're a vegan?" I repeat. Which is a mistake, because now Simone and Amelie hear what she said.

Amelie throws her hands in the air. "Amazing! I was worried I'd be a total outcast here."

"WAIT! Vegans can eat gluten, right?" Simone asks. We had a scarring experience a few years ago when her mom went gluten-free for weeks and stopped making Korean pancakes for us. Korean pancakes are actually called *jeon*, and they're delicious fried vegetable patties.

"Definitely," Amelie agrees. "Rice, potatoes, pasta, as long as it's made without eggs . . ."

Oh no. Korean pancakes have eggs.

"Well, then, consider me enrolled! This will be perfect, *mes amies*!" She obviously doesn't realize.

They all stare at me expectantly.

"Sounds great," I say.

We clink our water bottles together with a celebratory vegan cheer.

Eating less meat is good for the planet. And there's only one chunk of chicken left in my thermos, anyway. I push it deep beneath the noodles.

Fortunately for Simone, she's already finished her CoastFresh cheeseburger. I wonder if she knows it wasn't vegan. Cheeseburgers have always been her kryptonite.

6

Ventriloquist Act

In science on Thursday, Ms. Flores talks about the researchers who first tracked gene mutations. They studied fruit flies, which they kept inside old milk jars.

"That lab must have smelled disgusting," Amelie says.

"Actually, it was even worse than disgusting," Ms. Flores says. "Do you know what they fed the fruit flies?"

We obediently shake our heads.

"Rotten bananas."

"So horriblific," Simone says.

Reza makes barfing sounds.

"They discovered that white-eyed fruit flies pass their gene mutations from one generation to the next," Ms. Flores says, as if that discovery was worth years of sour milk and rotting bananas.

"In humans —"

I don't get to hear about humans, because a sixth-grader appears at our classroom door with a note. Ms. Flores reads it, then looks up.

"Simone and Emily L., Mr. Chadwick wants to borrow you for a few minutes. Apparently it's urgent."

When Simone raises her eyebrows at me, I shrug. I have no idea why he needs us.

"He can't have a question about the podcast," Simone says as we head for the library. "I haven't even recorded my parts yet."

"I checked that all the audio files were uploaded. And I printed the transcripts for him."

I proofread the transcripts twice. And I'm sure he wouldn't pull us from class to talk about a typo.

When we reach the library, Mr. Chadwick has one hand pressed to his jaw. His face is flushed.

"Toothache," he says, barely moving his lips. "Dentist appointment."

With his free hand, he stuffs papers into his briefcase. I move to hold it open for him but avert my eyes. Thinking about Mr. Chadwick at the dentist is almost as gross as thinking about fruit flies.

"That story about the march on October 29," Mr. Chadwick says. He sounds like the world's worst ventriloquist. "I ran it past the principal. He doesn't think it's a good idea."

As soon as he says the date, all I can think about is Asha Jamil's visit the day before. Asha Jamil! I have to force myself to focus.

"Did I get something wrong about the march?" I ask. Mya *was* talking at lightning speed, but I double-checked all her facts against the event listing.

Mr. Chadwick shakes his head. "The march is for high-school students. It might not be appropriate for Cedarview kids."

I tilt my head. What does that mean, exactly?

"Not appropriate?" Simone sounds equally confused.

"Can't have kids skipping school," he says. "Need to make good decisions."

Then he winces again. Grabbing a blank piece of paper, he starts writing.

Can't be seen as encouraging this. Why don't you create a bulletin board about climate issues? We can put it on display.

"A bulletin board," I say flatly.

Mr. Chadwick checks his watch.

Need to run. Sorry.

With that, he's out the door, leaving Simone and me alone in the library.

"I can't believe he's canceling my piece!" I fume.

"Is he allowed to? Just like that?" she asks.

"I don't know. He's the one in charge of the podcast. I guess he can make up whatever rules he wants." I slump into one of the chairs.

CENSORED: *The story of a silenced teen.*

I worked hard on that piece!

Because of the twisted laws of the universe, Principal Lau walks into the library and glares at us.

"What are you girls doing in here? Don't you have somewhere to be?" he says.

I jump up, banging my legs into the library table. It slides away with a screech.

"Sorry."

Simone follows me as I scurry past the principal and into the hall.

"Wait," she whispers. "Shouldn't we at least ask him about our climate march story?"

"It wasn't —"

It wasn't the right time. That's what I was about to say. But maybe it only feels like the wrong time because my hands are shaking and I can't figure out how to say anything politely.

"I need to decide on a strategy. Then we'll talk to him."

When we get back to the science room, everyone's hard at work.

"Thank goodness you're here. My head is buzzing," Daniella says as I sit down next to her. She's tracking fly mutations on what looks like a giant flowchart.

My head is positively buzzing too, and it has nothing to do with flies.

The rest of the class seems to last forever. I want to go home and scroll through a thousand YouHappy posts. Instead, I have to listen to Simone and Amelie whisper.

"This seems a *lot* like censorship —"

"I can go with you to talk to Mr. Lau and —"

"Emily, did you hear that? Amelie says —"

When I try to explain that I need time to come up with the best diplomatic approach, Ms. Flores appears over my desk.

"Something you want to share with the class, Emily?" she asks.

"Sorry, Ms. Flores."

I shake my head. I *never* get in trouble. This is entirely Amelie's fault.

I wonder what advice Emily Post would give in this situation. Unfortunately, she didn't write a chapter called "What to do when your podcast piece is canceled and people won't be quiet for long enough to let you think straight."

At least the bell is going to ring soon. I watch the minute hand on the classroom clock tick closer to freedom. Then, just before it gets there, the PA crackles.

"Students, be advised there is a media event in progress at the main entrance to the school. Please exit by the rear or side doors. We appreciate your cooperation."

At the words "media event" there's a burble of questions.

Ms. Flores holds up both hands. "No need to get involved. They're announcing some funding for the school." For some reason, she looks unhappy about the idea. "You'll probably see it on the city news tonight. In the meantime, stay out of the way," she says.

When the bell finally sounds, I leave class and file obediently out the south exit, following Daniella. Then Amelie plucks at my sleeve.

"C'mon," she says.

Simone stands beside her, looking torn. Her yellow scarf is askew, which I find strangely satisfying.

"Ms. Flores said to go straight home," I say.

Daniella says something too, but Amelie doesn't seem to hear either of us.

"Hurry up!" she orders.

Well, I'm not going to let her become the only one with the news. All of us hurry toward the front of the school.

I admit, I'm curious about the announcement. And the entire student body seems to have ignored instructions. There's a huge crowd gathered.

Parents have left their cars in the parking lot and joined the event. There's even a food truck here: The Tempeh Mobile. It idles at the edge of the street, across the grass.

What kind of announcement is this?

We find a spot along the edge of the action. Daniella looks as if she's going to hyperventilate, and for some reason even Amelie looks nervous now. She keeps glancing over her shoulder at the street.

At the top of the entranceway stairs, in front of the main double doors, the chair of the school board stands behind a podium. I've seen him before at a few of our assemblies. He has a bushy white mustache and eyebrows like toothbrush bristles. Today, he wears a black suit with a flashy blue shirt, the exact color of the CA Energy banner strung above his head. Beside him, there are two other men in business suits, along with Mr. Lau wearing his usual red tie.

Reporters hover near the base of the stairs, separated from the growing number of students by a line of yellow plastic tape.

Simone elbows me. "Look, that's Mya, the climate march organizer. You talked to her on the phone, right? She used to go here, to Cedarview."

I crane my neck to see a petite, dark-haired girl holding her phone toward the stage like a microphone.

Tap. Tap. Tap. Mr. School Board takes the microphone.

"Over the past five years, the school district has lost more than $20 million from its annual budget," he says.

Beside me, Simone muffles a sneeze.

"You okay?" Daniella whispers.

"I'm allergic to bad suits," Simone whispers back. "Oh, but my dad was showing me these designer Korean suits last night. If I don't go to Paris to become a designer, I might go to Seoul."

Unaware of Simone's fashion opinions, Mr. School Board continues to drone. "As you're aware, budgets are tight these days. At Cedarview Middle School alone, we've had to cut several teaching positions and delay technology purchases and facilities upgrades. But this week, we've signed an innovative agreement to help cover some of these losses. I'm pleased to introduce the publicity director of CA Energy, Mr. Chris Campbell, who will tell you more."

Another of the suited men steps to the podium, shaking Mr. School Board's hand as they trade places.

"He has the same last name as you!" Simone says to Daniella.

Daniella looks horrified.

Mr. Campbell has ginger hair, a bit long and tufty, as if he's a grown-up skateboarder. He wears wire-framed glasses, which he adjusts before he speaks.

"We at CA Energy are dedicated to educational opportunities. Education provides the ultimate key to our society's success, not to mention the development of our future workforce." He pauses to flash a toothpaste-white smile.

I spot Mya again, at the very front. Then the crowd shuffles and I lose sight of her.

"CA Energy is pleased to announce a $3million deal to build a new theater at Cedarview: the CA Energy Community Auditorium," Mr. Campbell continues. "During school hours, it will serve the needs of Cedarview students. Outside those hours, it will be utilized by CA Energy for our corporate events and used by the community." Another smile.

Simone turns toward me. Her eyes are wide like giant sequins, and I can tell exactly what she's thinking. She's about to say . . .

"We could have fashion shows!"

Daniella presses close against my side, as if she's trying to hide from this entire situation.

"He doesn't even like corporate events," she says.

"Who doesn't?"

"Where's Amelie?" Simone asks, at the same time.

"There." I spot her striding across the grass toward the street. Strange. Maybe she has a class right after school? Or a sudden craving for tempeh? The food truck is still there.

Simone shrugs, then presses closer to Daniella and me. She's trying to squeeze the three of us into a selfie. I smile obediently as Mr. Campbell continues speaking.

"I'll be pleased to answer any questions you might have about this exciting project."

The reporters surge forward as if he's a rock star and they might storm the stage. Mr. Campbell, his smile never wavering, calls on them one by one.

"We're discussing further investments, such as a scholarship fund for students," he tells one reporter.

"The partnership provides unique opportunities for both the company and the school," he tells another.

Then he calls on Mya. I stand on tiptoes, trying to see her better.

"Shouldn't education be fully funded by the government? Are corporate sponsorships not a —"

Mr. Campbell's smile slides sideways, as if he's tasted something sour. "This sponsorship agreement adheres to the highest ethical standards," he says. "We will be in no way interfering with education, sweetheart."

Another nod of his head to someone new.

Even from here, I can see Mya jumping up and down with her hand in the air, asking for a follow-up question. But Mr. Campbell ignores her.

"Uh-oh," Daniella murmurs.

She's right. Mya elbows her way through the crowd toward us. She's talking to a friend, and it seems as if steam should be coming out her ears.

"Arrogant . . . foot soldier of the patriarchy . . . so patronizing . . . didn't even get to ask my follow-up . . ."

Simone has been busy editing her photo and she seems to have missed the drama. She waves as Mya's about to stomp past us.

"Mya! This is my friend Emily, who interviewed you about the climate march. And this is Daniella. We're super excited about the march. And about the auditorium, because . . . fashion shows!"

Beside me, Daniella looks as if she'd like to disappear into a sinkhole. I can't blame her.

Mya's eyes slide over Simone, but she nods to me.

"You're the podcaster? Can't wait to hear your piece. Next month, maybe do a piece about corporations taking over public education?"

She shoots a glare over her shoulder at Mr. Campbell. "Can you believe he called me 'sweetheart'?"

"Well, actually, about my podcast piece —"

Her friend tugs at her. "Mya, I'm going to be late. And we don't need to re-educate everyone at this exact moment."

They head for the street.

I tried. I tried to tell Mya the climate march story wouldn't be running. And I'm sure one censored middle-school podcast piece won't affect the turnout for her event.

Back on stage, Mr. Lau takes the microphone.

"Thank you all for coming today. I know this will mark a new era for Cedarview Middle School, and I'm pleased that our students will benefit so greatly from the goodwill of CA Energy."

He smiles as he leaves the microphone for a round of handshakes.

Other students begin drifting past us. I tug Simone and Daniella toward the sidewalk.

"That was so dramatic." Simone sighs happily.

"Mya was dramatic," I say. "She's amazing."

"She's very brave," Daniella whispers.

"I'm sure she's right about corporate sponsorship and whatever." Simone sniffs. "But really, consider the possibilities. I have a vision, Emily. Fashion shows. Concerts."

She pauses. "Why did Amelie leave?"

I shrug. The food truck is gone too, so I may never learn the meaning of tempeh. But I have something more important to worry about.

"Simone, do you think Mr. Lau cut the story about the climate march because it might offend CA Energy?"

"What?" She looks as if I'm speaking a different language. One that's not French.

"CA Energy is an oil and gas company, right? So maybe a climate march —"

"Maybe they're a green energy company," Simone says.

Daniella shakes her head. "They're not."

"But they said, right up on stage . . . something about ethical standards."

Daniella looks doubtful.

"And an auditorium would be amazing," Simone continues. Then she gasps, grabbing Daniella's elbow. "Readings! We should have a talent show, and you can read from your poetry!" Simone's feet have stopped moving. She throws open her arms, as if conjuring us onto an invisible stage.

"You write poetry?" I ask Daniella. I had no idea.

She turns white. Even more white than usual. "Once. In seventh-grade English with Simone. But I mostly write code."

"Okay, don't panic," I tell her. "Auditoriums take a long time to build. We'll be in high school by the time it's ready."

Simone drops her arms, only to fling one of them around my shoulders.

"I am absolutely dreaming of the possibilities."

I sigh. I don't think this auditorium is going to change our lives. But I guess there's no harm in letting Simone hold on to her delusions.

7

Inapproprativeness

Simone stops by my house after the announcement. Once I've poured us each a bowl of corn chips (vegan!), we shut ourselves in my room and scroll through Asha's latest posts. We need to find a replacement piece for the podcast, but I'm not ready to think about it quite yet.

"We can easily do it later," Simone says.

"Absolutely. This is essential research," I agree, trying to crunch as politely as possible. It's sort of nice to put aside serious issues and scroll through gorgeous pictures for a while.

There are shots of Asha at a New York book launch, looking effortlessly glamorous in a raspberry-colored dress. In one photo she's signing a book, her head tilted to the side. Her long, dangly earrings sparkle against her dark hair. She's added the hashtags #CoconutLove and #EuforiaElle. Everyone knows that Asha loves EuforiaElle Coconut Bliss Shampoo.

I point to Asha's earrings. "She's worn those in at least three different posts. I think she has both gold and silver versions."

"I can't believe Mom won't buy me EuforiaElle products. They're not *that* expensive," Simone says.

"Why don't we both ask for the shampoo and conditioner for Christmas this year? And maybe for earrings like that, too."

Simone nods. "Stupendific idea."

"One day, we'll get all this stuff for free, because of my platform. And we can film hauls together. We'll include your fashion designs."

Influencers post their hauls all the time. When they get back from their shopping trips, they open their bags one by one and display what they've bought. Not all the "shopping trips" are real, because hardly any influencers actually *buy* the products. Once you have a few thousand followers, companies donate clothes and other products to add to your haul.

"I completely can't wait," Simone says.

Asha has also posted the most adorable pictures of her poodle, Lumpkin, along with a series of sunset views from her penthouse and one shot of the moon as seen from the International Space Station. And of course there are her daily posts about things we can do to make the world better.

This community orchard just opened in my neighborhood. A few years from now, we'll all be sharing its bounty! #Community #Sustainability #ChooseLove

The orchard is gorgeous, and her screen-printed CoastFresh shopping bags are cute, though I don't love the logo colors.

This is Margaret, who I met on the corner today. We split my sandwich, and it was the best lunch of my week. #MentalHealth #Addiction #ChooseLove

I expand her post to look at the photo more carefully.

"Do you think she actually had lunch with Margaret?"

Simone leans close to look. "The sidewalks look dirty and her jacket's a seriously light yellow. I don't think she would sit down there. Would you call that butter yellow or more sunshine yellow? It's in-between."

It sort of matches the yellow on the CoastFresh logo. I wonder if that's on purpose.

"I think she's faking this one," I say.

"But for a good reason. Whether or not she sat on the sidewalk, she's still supporting homelessness."

"She's supporting the unhoused," I clarify.

"That's what I said. Do you think —"

But I never get to hear what Simone might think, because Richard calls from downstairs.

"Girls, any chance you can help with something?"

When we emerge, he has hot chocolate waiting.

"This is fabulatastic," Simone says, and for once she's not exaggerating. It even has marshmallows.

"I have an ulterior motive," Richard says. "Your mom took Ocean to his karate class, and I want to hang some art before they get home. She'll be so happy if we get the last few things done around here. Can you be my advisers?"

This will delay our podcast planning, but Simone is already clapping her hands beside me.

"I adore surprises!" she says.

And it will be nice to do something for Mom. She has a string of huge weddings scheduled at the hotel this month. She's been working long hours and coming home exhausted. So even though more of our boxes are finally unpacked, the walls are still bare.

"Simone's a future fashion designer. She's good at this sort of thing," I say. Plus, Simone's house is sleek and modern, and I've always wished ours looked a little more like it.

Richard beams. "Simone, you can help us put soul into this place."

I don't believe that houses have souls. I'm clarifying this for the official record because I want NO BLAME for what happens on the walls of our townhouse.

Richard ushers us into the living room, where he's spread his art options across the floor. He's leaned Mom's various posters against the couch, in their pastel-colored plexiglass frames.

"Well, girls?" he asks. "Where shall we start?"

This is going to be a problem. Simone turns to me, eyes wide, and I can see she's reached the same conclusion.

Mom loves motivational phrases. Like, really loves them. In our Almond Park apartment there were posters everywhere. A kitten clinging to a table ledge with the words "Never Give Up!" A bright-blue underwater scene with starfish, sea urchins, and oysters that read "There's always a pearl." One summer, she hand-painted aspirational words onto our white kitchen tiles.

Emily Post said that some houses are only boring collections of furniture, while other houses — even if they aren't fancy — have a warm, inviting atmosphere. Our apartment definitely had . . . personality.

But now Richard's art is spread across the floor, and Richard has more international taste. If by "international" you mean a boat-shaped red lacquer . . .

"That's a harp," Richard says, when he sees me looking curiously at it.

Harp. And there's a pear-shaped Chinese vase and a plastic mask painted to look like wood.

"It's looking at me," I say.

"It's not authentic. I bought it downtown, because it reminds me of my dream to do a safari one day. I call him Fred." Richard grins.

"I call him creepy," Simone murmurs.

There are a dozen other questionable items on the floor, including a few more masks. One seems to be a lion with a blue tongue.

"Richard, could we please have a few extra marshmallows?" I ask. "I think that would help inspire us."

As soon as he leaves the room, Simone and I gape at one another. There is a distinct contrast between Fred and my mom's "Family Is Everything" poster featuring hedgehogs.

"I didn't know it would be this bad," I say.

"This is not bad. This is horrifically tragic. And tragically horrific," Simone says. "And I think it's cultural inappropriativeness, too."

"Cultural appropriation." I agree.

We did a whole unit about this at school last year. You can't just buy cultural artifacts from tourist stands and use them as decorations. You're basically buying stereotypes, and actual, authentic artists aren't getting the money. But apparently Richard didn't study this in seventh grade.

The soul of our house is in jeopardy.

My mom thought she found the perfect man . . . until THIS happened!

That would get a LOT of clicks. But I don't think I can share this situation with the world. It's way too embarrassing.

Richard returns, bearing steaming cups. "Two refilled hot chocolates, with additional marshmallows! I hope you don't mind drinking seconds. I still had lots left in the pot."

"Hot chocolate! Hot chocolate! Hot chocolate!" Ocean opens the front door just in time to hear the magic words. He barrels into the living room and straight into Richard's arms. "Did you make hot chocolate?"

"You're back early. Where's Susan?"

"She went to get groceries. She said she'll be here in half an hour."

"Okay, buddy. One more hot chocolate, coming right up."

"Hot chocolate! Hot chocolate!" Ocean seems as if he's already had a dozen cups, possibly laced with espresso. As soon as his dad disappears, he starts leaping through the minefield of artwork, using the open patches of floor like lily pads. When he hits the far wall, he turns around for another pass. "Hot chocolate! Hot chocolate!"

On his third trip through the art maze, Ocean misses.

"OOOOOOWWWWWWWWWWWWWWWW!"

The wail is only slightly louder than the splintering of wood as the lion's blue tongue snaps off, and the crack of a plastic frame as Ocean lands on Mom's ocean poster.

Richard rushes in. "What happened?"

"Mask disaster," Simone offers.

Ocean's wails drown out her words. Richard gathers him up and sits gingerly on the edge of the couch, beside the hedgehogs. "Sorry, buddy. You okay?"

"I wrecked the lion!"

"I know that's your favorite," Richard murmurs.

Simone and I glance at one another again. "Maybe he could play another round of hopscotch," Simone says under her breath. "Crack a few more?"

I have to bite my lip so I don't laugh out loud.

Eventually, Ocean calms down.

"Okay," Richard says, checking his watch. "We'd better get moving if we're going to surprise Susan."

"Richard," I say cautiously, "do you think these masks belong on our walls? We don't want to use stereotypes about other cultures as . . ."

"Casual decorations," Simone supplies, when I stumble.

"I see your point. But girls, these are just tourist stuff. They're not hurting anybody. And your mom loved them when she saw them in my old apartment."

"She did?"

"She said they were the most unique decorations she'd ever seen."

He grins so proudly, I can't bear to tell him Mom was probably being polite. "Unique" is not always a compliment.

Simone looks at me. I look at Simone. I can't see any way out of this. So I take our hot chocolate mugs to the safety of the kitchen. Then we get to work.

Simone decides we should hang all the masks in one corner of the entranceway. Richard agrees, and gets his tools.

"You can admire the collection as a whole this way," Simone tells him when he's done. I can practically imagine her dressed all in black, with wire-rimmed glasses on her nose, speaking to her future fashion clients.

"I love it," Richard says.

Designer Simone has other ideas, too. She returns to the living room to examine the poster options. "The kitten one is lovely, but the pink background clashes with the taupe of the living room walls. I suggest we hang it in the upstairs hallway."

"Do you think your mom will mind?" Richard asks me.

"Maybe you can choose new art for the living room. Together."

He nods enthusiastically. "Romantic. I like it."

Romantic. Or relationship-ending.

"This could be disastrous," I whisper, as Richard heads upstairs with the kitten. Ocean trots at his heels.

"What could go wrong?" Simone asks. "I'm sure the furniture stores are full of great possibilities. Like wooden masks with mottos."

At that moment, the front door opens. Something clunks to the floor. A sort of gasp-scream combination echoes from the foyer.

"Mom?"

"Honey?" Richard calls from upstairs.

We all rush to the entranceway. Mom stands there with

a hand on her heart. A grocery bag lies at her feet, apples spilling from it.

"You okay?" Richard asks.

She gives us a wavering smile. "Great," she says. "I just didn't expect the welcoming committee."

It's true, the masks seem to loom over her.

"Is this one . . . plastic?"

"His name's Fred," Ocean says.

She shifts her gaze to me, as if hoping I'll come up with reasons why it's a bad idea to hang plastic masks by the front door. But it wasn't me who decided to move in with Richard and Ocean. If she'd been thinking realistically, she might have considered the downsides before now.

"Welcome home," Richard says. "We thought we'd surprise you by getting some of the decorating done."

"Surprise!" Mom says weakly.

"I have your posters out, too," Richard says.

"Did you put the ocean in the living room?"

"About that . . . there was a slight accident."

"With my ocean poster?" Mom maintains a polite smile, but she doesn't sound happy.

"Well, I'd better go," Simone says. "Bye, Ms. Laurence! Thanks for the hot chocolate, Richard. Nice to see you, Ocean!"

"Wait," Richard says. "What was that thing about the pink and the taupe?"

But she's out the door, leaving the four of us to stare at one another.

The nine of us, if you count the masks.

8

Selfie Sabotage

I set the table for dinner. I'm about to ask if it's a vegan meal — I really need to talk to Richard about the whole vegan thing — but Mom's in the kitchen gluing the frame of her broken ocean poster, and Richard's making apologetic cooing noises.

He sounds like a pigeon.

I don't want to interrupt them, so I sit in the living room and scroll through Asha's YouHappy feed, reposting her suggestions to save plastic by using shampoo bars instead of bottles. I should get a shampoo bar, immediately, and then take a picture of it and tag Asha. I wonder if she'd notice. If she did, we'd be online friends even before she arrives at Cedarview.

I wonder if Asha would have advice about my climate march story. Obviously, she has to balance her own content with the views of her sponsors. Maybe she has strategies.

If we were friends, even online friends, I could ask her.

I consider unfriending her, then re-friending her, in hopes she'll suddenly notice my name and start following my account. But it seems like an immature strategy. And she probably doesn't scroll through her follows every day like I do. She has millions of people looking at her posts. She can't keep track of every single one.

What I need is for one of my posts to go viral and catch her attention. But that seems impossible when I only have thirty people looking at my account.

Ooh . . . make that thirty-two people. I have new followers! One of them is Amelie, and one is a person with no bio, who is apparently from Dubai. They don't have their picture uploaded, which seems sketchy.

I seem sketchy! I don't have my picture in my bio, because of Mom's outdated social media rules. That's probably why people don't follow me.

I really, really need to be able to post pictures of myself. I'm going to convince her to change her mind. Immediately.

I head for the kitchen, but Richard and Mom have both disappeared.

I find Mom first. She's outside on the sidewalk, chatting with our neighbor.

"Sorry Simone had to leave," she says, when I join them. Her last word is basically drowned out by the hollering of Ocean and Jackson as they zoom past us on the sidewalk, Ocean clinging to the back of Jackson's motorized wheelchair.

"He got a new chair yesterday," Jackson's mom says. "He's a little excited."

They're ridiculously loud. Someone might call the police about a neighborhood disturbance.

"I'm so glad these two found each other," she says.

I nod politely, but I'm not sure the rest of the world would agree. They seem like an evil uprising in the making.

"Should we slow them down?" Mom asks. "I don't want Jackson to get hurt."

"But it's good to see them having fun together," his mom says. "Let's give them another five minutes."

Five more minutes of mayhem. But maybe this is my chance. I wait for a slight decrease in noise level.

"Mom, you remember how Asha Jamil is coming to Cedarview?"

"Who?"

I refrain from scowling. I told her everything about the visit, but she and Richard were trying to figure out how to share closet space at the time and I *knew* she wasn't properly listening to me. Also, Richard has a lot of gray T-shirts.

The boys whip by in the opposite direction, screaming as if they're on a roller coaster.

"Is Asha Jamil the one who played the astronaut on that show?" Jackson's mom says.

There's hope for her.

"She's coming to my school, and I'll probably get to give her a tour."

"That's wonder —"

The boys zoom toward us again. Before Jackson's mom can finish her sentence, the chair touches the edge of the curb.

It wobbles.

Both moms gasp. Their hands fly to their hearts.

The chair tilts from the curb.

And then . . .

BOOM!

The sound of the wheelchair smashing onto the road echoes down the street. Before I can react, the moms race for the crash scene.

I am never going to get any attention around here.

I stomp over to see if anyone needs hospitalization. When I get there, the moms are struggling to right the chair, which seems mostly intact. I help them get it back on the sidewalk, where both boys are sitting on their butts, laughing their heads off.

"Jackson," his mom grunts. "This is no laughing matter. I want you to have fun, but this chair is worth as much as our car."

"But —"

"No buts."

As the boys burst into another round of laughter, the moms look at each other in confusion.

"You said *butts*," I clarify.

The boys laugh harder. The moms are still confused.

"Ocean!" Mom says, in her best parent-voice. The one that would make me snap to attention. It stifles the laughter only a little.

Ocean's palms are bleeding. Jackson has a scraped elbow and a slightly bloody knee. He seems otherwise fine. After a few minutes, his mom helps boost him into his slightly dented chair.

Jackson and his mom head toward their townhouse door, a lecture on safety drifting behind them. My mom takes Ocean firmly by the elbow until we're inside.

"Jackson has cerebral palsy," Ocean says. "That means his legs don't work quite right, but his brain works fine. I asked."

"Ocean . . ." Mom starts, looking as if she has a sudden headache.

"What?"

She sighs. "Let's be quiet for a few minutes, okay?"

"I can be quiet for a long time. Dad usually pays me a dollar, though."

"Fine."

He falls mercifully silent.

Which makes me wonder. Did Mom mean that we should *all* be quiet, or just that Ocean should stop talking? Because I never did get to ask my question. And it's not as if she's offering me any money.

I decide to risk it.

"Mom, a few students will probably meet Asha Jamil in person. I'll almost for sure be one of them. Two weeks from today, I'll be meeting her. And I might need to ask her for advice even before that."

"That's great, Em."

"So I'd like to tag her in some selfies, starting now, and establish a basis for our relationship."

Mom looks just as confused as she did about the butts. "What?"

"I need a way to get her attention, so I can ask her for advice. And this is a potential step forward in my career."

"Your career," she says flatly.

While we stand in the hallway talking, Ocean inches slowly toward the stairs.

"My career as an influencer. I mean, that's not my main reason for asking, but if I post selfies with some of the products that Asha promotes..."

Ocean lunges for freedom. Just in time, Mom grabs the back of his shirt. She's surprisingly fast.

"You. Stay put," she tells him.

"You." She transfers her finger-point toward me. "Absolutely no selfies until high school. At *least* until high school. If you meet Asha, you can talk to her in person."

Back to Ocean. "Let's clean those cuts on your hands and find your father. Now."

That's it. They're gone. And not only did Mom once again misguidedly forbid me to post proper pictures, she said "*if*" I meet Asha. IF!

How I climbed the ladder to international influence without one drop of family support.

It's unfortunate, really. Although it will make a dramatic podcast episode or video series in the future. Viewers love when you post about obstacles in your personal life.

"It took me an entire week to win her over," I'll say. "I had to choose every moment wisely."

The story will be extra inspiring.

If I ever manage to convince her.

9

Moving to Mars

As soon as I get to school on Friday morning, I march directly to the library.

Last night, Richard watched a documentary about severe weather caused by climate change. And even though I was doing homework and not actually watching, I heard enough. Enough to make me wake up in the middle of the night worrying about hurricanes. Then, since I was already awake, I spent some time stewing about my lack of social media influence and my failure on the climate march story.

At this rate, I'll be a hundred years old before I have enough influence to make people wear hoop earrings, let alone march to save the Earth. Forest fires and mega-storms will destroy everything while I'm scheduling stories about cafeteria rats.

Censoring our podcast is *so* not fair! Telling people about climate action is NOT the same as telling them to skip school to buy slushies. Plus, Mr. Chadwick is a librarian. Isn't he supposed to be all about free speech and the exchange of ideas?

That's exactly what I'm going to tell him. Politely.

It's possible I got even less sleep than I thought, because I march straight up to his desk and start talking without properly looking at him.

"Excuse me, Mr. Chadwick, I've been thinking and thinking, and I believe it's unfair that you cut the climate march story and —"

I stutter to a stop, because as Mr. Chadwick leans forward, Ms. Flores *also* leans forward. From her chair behind the library desk, right next to Mr. Chadwick's chair. RIGHT next to it. Did they just move their arms? Were they HOLDING HANDS before I got here? Simone's theory about the two of them rushes back to me, and I feel my cheeks turning red.

"Um... sorry... I just wanted to talk about... I'll come back..."

"Did you say 'climate march story'?" Ms. Flores asks.

Well, I suppose she should know everything about the person she's flirting with. Otherwise, she might find out he has a bathroom-stinker-upper of a son after she's already moved in.

"I wrote a story about the climate march, but we can't include it in the podcast because it might encourage kids to skip school."

Ms. Flores raises her eyebrows, glancing back at Mr. Chadwick.

He murmurs something. I think he says the principal's name.

"This wouldn't have anything to do with the sponsorship agreement, I imagine?" Ms. Flores says, in a tone that suggests it's exactly what she's imagining.

"That's what *I* wondered!" I blurt.

"I admit, the timing is questionable," Mr. Chadwick says. "But Mr. Lau does have a point. These are younger kids we're talking about. And our podcast is on shaky ground. The budget . . ."

"Hmmm," Ms. Flores says.

Some people have the ability to put a lot of meaning into a single sound.

She gets up from the desk.

"Thanks for the coffee, Hugh," she says.

(Who knew Mr. Chadwick's first name was *Hugh*?)

Then she taps me on the shoulder as she passes.

"Keep fighting the good fight," she says.

Mr. Chadwick doesn't look at all happy when she's gone.

"Sorry I interrupted your date," I say.

"It wasn't a —" He stops, with a small sigh. "What would you like me to do?"

Hope blooms in me. "Put the climate march piece back in the lineup for next week's episode!"

But he's already shaking his head.

"Could you please talk to Mr. Lau about it?" I try.

He shakes his head again. "You'll have a better chance than me with that idea. Why don't you try?"

I gape at him. From the tank next to his desk, Persephone the goldfish gapes at both of us.

I came here so I wouldn't need to talk to Mr. Lau. I really don't want to talk to the principal. And no one told me the producer position would be nearly this much trouble.

For the rest of the morning, I imagine scenes in which I convince Mr. Lau to let my climate march story stay in the podcast lineup. In some of these scenes, I'm so persuasive that he cancels school for the day of the march and encourages everyone to attend.

Which doesn't seem exactly realistic.

"We'll figure something out," Simone whispers, while we're doing math worksheets. "I'll come with you."

"That would be so good," I tell her.

But I still need something perfectly influential to say. Something to convince him that the climate's more important than CA Energy.

When the bell rings, I get distracted by another problem. Richard sent me a ham sandwich for lunch. It's some sort of gourmet ham sandwich with pineapple chutney, but there's no disguising the fact that it's meat. I never did talk to him about the vegan thing. I'm serious about protecting the environment, but his ham dinner last night was *really* good. When I saw him put the sandwich into my lunch bag this morning, I considered asking for carrot sticks or something instead. And then I didn't. Because who wants to eat carrot sticks for lunch?

I'm a terrible vegan.

No, I'm not. I'm simply in a transition phase. But I'm going to need a different place to eat my lunch today.

I grab my bag from my locker while Simone and Amelie are in the bathroom. Together. Then I check to make sure there are no clandestine dates happening at the check-out desk of the library (none, thank goodness) and I retreat to the reading corner. Along the way, I pick up a hardcover book about dinosaurs, for camouflage.

Two minutes later, I've claimed the plush chair behind the fish tank. I pull one of the beanbag chairs over to serve as a footrest, then curl up with my book propped open on my lap and my phone and lunch bag hidden behind it. Even if Mr. Chadwick pokes his nose into this corner, he'll only see dinosaurs. I perfected this strategy in sixth grade, after I threw up after a pizza lunch and the pizza was still recognizable. I couldn't show my face in the cafeteria for a week.

As I sink my teeth into my sandwich (it's spectacularly delicious), I check on Asha's day. She's shopping for sustainable fashion, exactly the type of clothing that Simone wants to design. My favorite item is a soft gray skirt that swirls around her when she moves, but even that is not half as nice as what Simone draws in her sketchbook.

I click the reply button.

@realAshaJamil, just wait until you see what my friend @SustainableSimone designs once she launches her own line. You'll be over the moon and back again!

That last line is an in-joke used by Asha's followers, because of her outer space TV experience.

Actually, I'm wearing a ring that Simone made herself in a jewelry class last year. I hold it near my face and snap a selfie. Then I type a caption, just to see what it would look like if I were allowed to post photos of myself.

@realAshaJamil, here's a @SustainableSimone design that's my absolute favorite.

I'm about to delete the draft when I hear a rustle. I peek over the edge of my dinosaur book, on alert for Mr. Chadwick, but it's only Marcus. He's wearing a lab coat with a polka-dot handkerchief poking from the pocket.

"I like the fashion statement," I tell him. "What are you doing?"

He takes a step closer and peers over the edge of the book. I grab at my sandwich, to whisk it back into my lunch bag, but I accidentally hit my phone instead. And when I touch the screen, my thumb brushes the post button.

"Oh no!"

"What?" Marcus asks, eyes wide.

"I posted something on YouHappy."

"Something bad?"

"No . . . not exactly."

My stomach cramps, the way it did when I spilled juice on our couch in third grade and tried to cover it up by flipping the cushion.

Then, after a minute, the cramp passes. Is this really such a terrible thing? It's probably not what I would have chosen for my first-ever appearance in a YouHappy post, but it's also not the worst option. And if Mom notices, I'll simply explain what happened. Besides, she looked at my phone last week. She probably won't check again for ages.

I look more closely at Marcus.

"Why the lab coat, Marcus?"

"I'm a scientist. Would you consider moving to Mars?" he asks.

I notice he's holding the copy of Asha's book, the one I gave him last time we were in the library.

"Isn't it a little barren? No air. No trees. No malls."

He flops onto a beanbag chair. "I know. But I don't see how we're going to survive here."

"Survive what?"

"COMPLETE CLIMATE DISASTER!" He jabs a finger at his book.

Marcus isn't great at eye contact. He seems to be staring across the reading area toward Persephone in the fish tank.

I set my lunch bag and dinosaur book to one side.

"There's still time to make things better here. A bit of time."

"But we're not *doing* anything," he says. "I looked it up, and everything's getting worse."

This is true. I scrape my brain, looking for something hopeful, but I find only forest fires and hurricanes.

"We need to do something RIGHT NOW," Marcus says. More finger jabbing. More fish tank staring. Persephone stares back at us, stunned by the hopelessness of it all.

"EVERYONE has to change EVERYTHING."

This seems a bit of a reach. Although . . . there is *something* we can do.

"Marcus, do you know what an influencer is?"

He shakes his head.

"It's someone who uses social media to change the way people think. And that's what I'm going to be, as soon as I'm allowed to include photos in my posts."

"You'd better get started," he says.

"Well, I can't, because my mom thinks we live in the 1800s or something."

He looks confused.

"But there are other people using their influence right now!" I say. "Remember how Asha Jamil's coming to visit Cedarview? She's working to convince people to save the Earth. And I'm going to be like that."

"An actor?"

"Well, no. Asha has influence because she's such a famous actor. I'm going to have influence because I'm an influencer."

He seems confused again, but I feel a sudden swell of hope. This is what I've been missing: the connection between climate change and my role as an influencer. Of course! This will be my Big Issue. I'll be an influencer who looks at everything — fashion, cooking, interior design — through the lens of environmental change. In a positive way, of course. This will give my social media profiles more focus. It will inspire followers. It will link seamlessly to Simone's sustainable fashion brand.

I found my calling as an influencer when I was still in middle school. Here's how it happened . . .

I'll be even more powerful than The Palette Pixie.

Or The Palette Pixie and I could collaborate! Sometimes, influencers work in groups. They like each other's material, repost, and do channel takeovers. It's a good strategy, because the whole influencer thing is all about math. The algorithms (those are the math formulas) boost posts with lots of likes and shares. When influencers team up, they can make each other more popular.

I have another brain wave. If I adopt climate change as my major issue, Amelie's vegan club will seem like a small, lesser branch of my empire. She'll be a little puddle under my giant climate-action umbrella.

This is brilliant! I could hug Marcus right now, except I'm pretty sure that would scare him. But I want to do something nice for him.

"Marcus, you know about Greta Thunberg, right? She's on the autism spectrum. She has her own book about saving the Earth."

"I could be interested."

"I'll find it for you."

Unfortunately, just as I'm about to search for the book, Rob shows up.

"MARCUS!"

Marcus and I must look at him with matching startled faces. Rob lowers his volume.

"I've been searching everywhere for you. You have a doctor's appointment. You're supposed to meet your mom outside."

Marcus sighs as if he's a hundred years old.

"I'd like to use my influence to fix climate change and eliminate doctors," he says.

"I'll make those two of my first campaigns, once I'm a professional," I promise.

As they leave, Rob turns back to thank me, as if I single-handedly found Marcus and saved his day. But really, Marcus just saved mine.

10

Accidental Water Fight

On Saturday morning, I click the heart button on three of Asha's posts — one about her poodle, one about how to properly wear a knitted hat with your hair framing your face, and one about the sustainable silk sheets she just bought. She says she's only sleeping on silk for the rest of her life.

Our landline rings, and Richard bellows up the stairs at Ocean.

"Your mom's on the phone!"

Ocean barrels down. His chattering echoes through the house. Apparently, he has a lot of updates for his mom and a lot of questions about L.A.

It's almost impossible to concentrate in this house. But just as I'm about to close my YouHappy app, I notice Simone has reposted something from Amelie.

Vegan French Toast — you'd never know it was coconut milk.

Simone says she's going to try it tomorrow. Since when does Simone cook? First she turns French, and now she's a vegan chef? Daniella has already liked the post. Muttering to myself, I add my own heart, so they don't think I'm ignoring them.

While I think of it, I message Daniella.

Did you talk to Bryce?

She replies quickly.

I talked to Mr. Chadwick, without giving him
names. He said I should be more assertive.

This is probably good advice, but I'm not sure how assertive Daniella can get.

What else?

He said boys this age sometimes express
themselves strangely, and Bryce might . . . like me.

Gross!

Obviously, Mr. Chadwick is no help in this situation.

So what are you going to do?

But Daniella doesn't answer. Maybe she's doing homework or something.

After a minute, I toss my phone to the side and start making notes for my meeting with Mr. Lau, which I am absolutely, definitely going to have on Monday morning.

1. Be polite but firm.
2.
3.

When I can't think of anything else, I go to the expert. I pull Emily Post's *Etiquette* from my shelf and flip to the section on business. (Unfortunately, Emily Post didn't write any chapters about middle school.)

She says that when you're having a business meeting, you shouldn't sit with your feet on your desk and a newspaper spread in your lap. That doesn't seem applicable. She also says it's good to appear polished. "One advantage of polish is that one's opponent can never tell what is going on under the glazed surface of highly finished manners."

I'm not entirely sure what she means. Still, I write it down.

2. Be polished.

This isn't going to help me. I guess the only thing left for my list is:

3. Convince Mr. Lau that climate marches are good and censorship is bad.

It's lucky I have the rest of the weekend to work out the details.

Sighing, I close my notebook and log onto YouHappy again. There's a new video from The Palette Pixie, offering her best tips on how to make your influence last.

It's exactly what I need.

I'm making notes on how to develop my brand identity when Mom pops her head into my room.

"Can you watch Ocean for a little while?" she asks. "I want to get to the store before it closes, so Richard can see the lamps I found."

Babysitting is not AT ALL part of my brand identity.

"I have a lot of work to do," I say.

Mainly, I have to finish my notes. Then I'm going to call Simone, because we need to talk about what we'll tell Asha about our lives. And I should remind her about our podcast recording session.

Mom is unconvinced. "Ocean can entertain himself. Just keep an eye out. I don't want a repeat of that wheelchair race with Jackson."

"Fine." I suppose I can manage that, even while planning my sparkling future.

But then she ambushes me.

"Oh, and run the vacuum around, will you?"

Before I can protest, she disappears from my doorway. And by the time I drag myself off the bed, she and Richard are practically out the door. It's as if they've learned to teleport.

"Love you." Mom waves.

Then they're gone.

Just got left with vacuuming AND babysitting duties. On a Saturday!

I post this along with a gif of Cinderella's pumpkin-coach.

Unfortunately, there's not a fairy godmother in sight. Just Ocean, jumping up and down in front of me like a labradoodle.

"What are we going to do? What are we going to do?"

I put my phone away. "*You* are going to entertain yourself. *I'm* going to vacuum."

His face falls, and I feel a momentary . . . something. A pang of sibling responsibility? Probably just indigestion.

"Maybe we can play a game," I say reluctantly. "But I really do have to vacuum first."

"Great! I'll get the iPad," he says. Then he's off, running to his room. "I have a game with vampires and werewolves. You can be the werewolf!"

He'll probably have nightmares. Then Mom and Richard will be sorry.

I have a lot of time to appreciate the multiple levels of our townhouse as I drag the vacuum up and down the stairs. But at least I can think while I work. When I'm famous and I live in a penthouse, my apartment will have a special elevator so the butler can collect my nightly meal delivery. Then I'll have no need for a kitchen. And of course Simone will live one floor down, so she can join me for dinner each evening.

I lug the vacuum to the basement bedroom. Ocean is already there, the iPad near his feet. He's standing at the door to the en suite bathroom, flicking the lights on and off.

I know what he's looking at. The previous tenants installed a "Parisian bidet" (rental ad) or "butt-washer" (Richard's term). It's not a real bidet. It's an attachment that sits on top of the toilet, instead of the usual toilet seat. There's a small plastic pocket mounted on the wall beside it, holding a remote control.

What kind of toilet seat has a remote control? And why would a toilet seat need so many buttons? I've read that bidets are environmentally friendly, but...

"Let's try it," Ocean calls, over the noise of the vacuum.

I ignore him.

"C'mon, Emily. Just once," he says.

I make perfect lines across the bedroom carpet. Then I turn off the vacuum and stand beside Ocean at the threshold to the bathroom. The whole decor looks wacky. There are gold turtles on the wallpaper and tiny gold ducks on the orange tiles over the sink. This is the weirdest, most embarrassing room in the townhouse.

"I'm gonna do it," Ocean says. "I'm going to use the butt-washer."

"You are not!"

He slips into the bathroom and shuts the door in my face. A minute later, I hear him peeing. Next he yelps. Then he starts laughing hysterically. While he's still doing up his pants, and definitely before he's had time to properly wash his hands, he whips open the door and tries to push me inside.

"Emily, you have to try it."

"Why? Why do I have to?"

"It's good to have new experiences," he says. This is something my mom says all the time. Apparently, we're rubbing off on him.

"I'm satisfied with my usual experience."

"Dad says they use bidets in Asia and Europe."

This makes me hesitate. Simone says her grandma has a bidet in her house in Korea, so Simone must already know how to use one. Amelie was probably born knowing exactly how to use anything Parisian. When I'm a famous influencer and Simone's a fashion designer, traveling will be one of our most fabulous talents. London, Berlin, Paris, Hong Kong. Those places are bound to be ultra sophisticated, and cross-cultural exposure could be a useful thing.

My pause gives Ocean enough time to push me inside the room, slam the door, and lean against it. He may be five years younger than me, but he's freakishly strong.

"I'm not letting you out until you try it!" he says.

Which, because of the whole furniture store and lamp thing, means I could be stuck in here for hours.

It's a serious conundrum.

I pound on the door, but Ocean won't budge.

"Try it!" he yells.

"Let me out of here right this second!"

"No!"

Mom should have introduced Richard to Emily Post's advice books much, much earlier. Emily Post has extremely useful thoughts on parenting. For example, she says: "Any child can be taught to be beautifully behaved with no effort greater than quiet patience and perseverance, whereas to break bad habits once they are acquired is a Herculean task."

Ocean's bad habits are significant.

"Open it! Now!"

"No!"

It goes on like this for a while, until I give up.

It feels like the wallpaper turtles are watching me. But I really do have to pee.

The seat's cushioned. And warm. And environmentally friendly, I remind myself.

An electronically heated seat seems like a major electrocution risk, but I pee anyway. Then I pull the remote control from its pocket and push "Auto."

I scream.

Water — COLD water — is hitting me IN PLACES WHERE WATER IS NOT SUPPOSED TO GO.

"How do I turn it off? How do I turn it off?"

"It turns off automatically!" Ocean yells.

"It's not! It's not stopping!"

I'm trapped in a semi-naked water-gun fight with a toilet. This is not good. This is the least good situation I've ever experienced. And when people say "cross-cultural exposure" this is NOT what they mean.

"Why won't it stop?"

"Do you want me to come in?" Ocean asks.

"No!"

"Do you want me to call my dad?"

"NO!"

"What are you going to do, then?"

This is an excellent question. If I stay, I'm going to get filled with water from the bottom up until I'm a giant balloon and then I'll probably pop and get put in the newspaper as the first-ever casualty of a Parisian Bidet, With Heated Seat Pad and Remote Control! But if I stand up, water's going to spray all over the entire bathroom. By the time Mom and Richard get home, Ocean and I will be paddling around in a rowboat with the turtles and ducks, trying to explain that I broke the toilet while attempting to prepare for my European future.

Meanwhile, my private parts are freezing. FREEZING!

I have to do something.

I stand up.

And the water stops.

"It stopped!" I call through the door, thinking Ocean will be relieved to avoid the whole rowboat scenario. But once I remember how to breathe, adjust my clothes, and wash my hands, I find him lying on the carpet outside. He's laughing so hard there are tears streaming down his face. If he hadn't just gone pee, I'm sure he would have wet his pants.

"Don't you know how to use a remote control?" he gasps. "You're lucky I didn't have a heart attack."

He doesn't care. "That was the funniest . . . the funniest thing . . ."

I lean over him. "If you ever tell ANYONE about this —"

"Are you kidding? I'm telling EVERYONE! And I recorded you on the iPad so they can hear it for themselves."

The icy feeling that flows through me at this moment is even worse than the cold of the bidet. I stare at Ocean. He's managed to haul himself into a sitting position, but he's still laughing.

"Delete that recording, and I'll play your werewolf game for as long as you want."

No response.

"And I'll give you ten dollars."

I've been saving for a ring light, to properly illuminate my features in future YouHappy videos. Losing ten dollars is going to delay my purchase, but this is an emergency.

Ocean has stopped laughing. He tilts his head to one side. "But I could play this for Dad, and your mom. And I could tell Jackson..."

I can't think of anything worse than two eight-year-old delinquents discussing my bidet experience. Nothing.

"Fifteen dollars," I say.

"AND you owe me something."

"What?"

"I don't know yet. But I'll tell you when I need it."

Small boy is secretly a mafia boss. Find out how he did it.

Great. I live with a tiny criminal mastermind. Still, what choice do I have?

"Fine."

"Deal?"

"Deal."

"But that was hilarious," he says. "You sounded so funny. *How do I turn it off? How do I turn it off?*"

I watch him click the delete button on his tablet. Then I grit my teeth and stomp to the stairs, grabbing the vacuum on my way. When I look back, Ocean's still giggling.

He looks like a cherub from one of those church-ceiling paintings, which makes the whole situation even worse.

11

Girl Time

Early on Sunday morning, Mom and I set off for The Allegra, where she works. In the Opus Café, near the lobby, I order a white chocolate mocha with a tower of whipped cream — one of their specialties.

I've been worried Mom might cancel on me again this week, but she seems happy to be out of the house. I don't think she heard about the bidet incident, either.

Once we have our drinks (Mom orders an ultra-boring Americano), we head for the elevators. The doors slide open and a group of four women gets out in a cloud of perfume and an entire forest's worth of fur. One has a thick, furry scarf (a mink?) wrapped around her neck. I think it has teeth.

"Is that real?" I whisper.

Mom gives me an almost imperceptible nod.

Thank goodness Amelie's not here to have an aneurysm.

"Who were they?" I ask as the group disappears through the lobby.

"That's the opera star Evelyn Montague and her team. She's the one with the fur collar. Do you know she travels with her own naturopath?" Mom grins.

As the brass doors close behind us, Mom clicks her access card against the security panel and I press the button for the fourth floor.

The Allegra has tons of celebrity guests. It's not as posh as some of the hotels downtown, but Mom and the rest of the staff try really hard to make everyone feel at home. Mom says it's a "boutique experience." And everyone who works here is amazing. When I was small, Howard, the security manager, used to run me up and down an empty hallway while I clung to the top of a luggage cart. And I used to visit the laundry room and breathe in the steam and fabric softener while I "helped" fold towels.

We see Janina, the head of housekeeping, as we step out of the elevator. She grabs my face and kisses my cheeks before I can even say hello.

"Taller every time you come!" she says. She slips me a handful of foil-wrapped chocolates from her apron pocket.

Once she and Mom have finished discussing how brilliant I am (so embarrassing), we make our way along paisley carpet and past elaborately carved doorframes. Inside Mom's office, she sits at her desk while I curl up on the plush, emerald-green couch along the far wall. It has scrolled woodwork on the armrests, as if it might have come straight from a French mansion. This is absolutely the most romantic place to imagine writing my future bestsellers, once I'm famous.

I take a deep breath. In here, I can forget about Ocean and the bidet scene altogether. The whipped cream on my mocha smooths away all the annoying things Amelie did this week. And the sprinkle of cinnamon on top is almost enough to make me forget the way Mom is blocking my selfie plans.

"Do you have homework to do this morning?" Mom asks, as she settles herself at the computer.

"Yup. Just getting started."

Last night, as I was falling asleep, I had a podcast idea that's going to be the utmost in sneaky perfection. It will be a story about the climate march, but it will be disguised as part of my own advice segment. (In one of the most famous episodes of *Outer Orbit*, Asha Jamil's character sends a message in secret code to Earth from the International Space Station so news of an approaching asteroid doesn't scare the other astronauts. I feel as if Asha would fully approve of my new plan.)

I pull out my notebook and start writing.

EMILY: What's next in our episode, Simone?

SIMONE: Well, Emily, we've received a tricky question from one of our listeners. Here's what it says:

Dear Cedarview Speaks:
I try to be a good person. I really do.
But what happens when doing something good means breaking the rules? Purely hypothetically, this good thing could be . . .

for example . . . attending an event for climate action when I'm supposed to be in school. If it's a good cause, does that make it okay to break the rules?

Signed, In a Tizzy

EMILY: What a great question, Simone! To answer it, I had to go all the way back to the 1920s and the advice of Emily Post, the queen of etiquette.

SIMONE: Emily Post had advice about climate action?

EMILY: Well, no. She wasn't super aware of things like environmentalism or anti-racism or social justice, like you and I are today.

SIMONE: So what did she say? What should poor Tizzy do about her situation?

EMILY: Emily Post believed etiquette was about more than using the right fork. It was about ethics and honor.

SIMONE: Um . . . what does that mean, exactly? Tizzy's not asking what fork to use.

EMILY: But she *is* asking about rules that don't make sense. When something is as big and important as climate change, the small things — like using the right fork, or missing a single Friday-afternoon science class — don't seem as important.

SIMONE: Emily, you are a wonder. Both of you!

EMILY: Always happy to help. Tizzy, get out there and change the world!

It takes me a few drafts, and my mocha is long gone before the script strikes the perfect balance between innocence and school absenteeism. But when I'm finished, I find myself smiling at my own scribbles. This is the benefit of writing the questions *and* the answers for my monthly podcast segment. I can give advice to myself! Or at least listen to Emily Post's advice. And she was entirely right. I can't let Mr. Lau's rules get in the way of climate action and my future as an environmentally focused influencer.

I bet Mr. Chadwick doesn't even read my advice segment transcripts. He probably won't notice the climate march reference.

I look up from my notebook.

"Mom, you know how I was writing about the climate march a few days ago?"

She glances away from her computer. "Of course."

"Can I go to that? It's in twelve days. Friday, October 29. Simone and I could leave school after lunch and walk downtown together. And I'll take my phone."

"Counting the days? Sounds like someone's excited."

Ignoring the slightly patronizing tone, I wait...

"I wonder if Ocean would want to join you. I could come along. It wouldn't kill me to take an afternoon off."

My eyes widen. It's as if each of her sentences has made the situation worse.

"I don't think you need to come," I say, in as polite a tone as humanly possible.

And then it happens again.

"I'll talk to Richard once we're home. Should we get going? The boys will want to do something outside this afternoon. Or maybe you can plan something with Ocean?"

Or maybe I absolutely can't.

"I bet he'd love to make signs for the march!" Mom smiles as if it's a brilliant idea.

I sigh. Emily Post has no advice about middle school and not a drop of advice about eight-year-old pseudo-brothers, either. I've already looked. This is the first time she's failed me. (Well, she also said that girls should always wear skirts and never pants. But she lived a *reeeally* long time ago.)

Thankfully, Ocean is already playing at Jackson's house when we get home from the hotel. I don't even have to see him until dinnertime.

When we sit down to eat, I try to tell Mom and Richard more about my plans for giving Asha Jamil the perfect school tour, and also convince them to lift Mom's unreasonable restrictions on my YouHappy account.

"I finished a new podcast script, too. I found a different way of talking about the climate march," I tell them.

Oops. I pause, holding my breath in case they ask why I need to talk about it in "a different way." I haven't exactly mentioned Mr. Lau's feelings about the podcast giving people the idea to skip school next Friday. Fortunately, everyone's distracted by their first bites of Richard's shepherd's pie. (It isn't at all like disgusting store-bought shepherd's pie. This one is delicious.)

"The march is going to be such a good opportunity to take photos. It would be great to show myself getting involved in —"

"Interesting," Mom says. "Ocean, don't forget your eye appointment tomorrow. I'm picking you up from school."

I'm displeased by the interruption, but Ocean looks even more displeased by the eye appointment idea. As Mom reaches for her water, he splats his fork into his mashed potato pie topping, sending a glob of it flying through the air to land on Mom's wrist. She jumps, knocking her glass over and spilling water onto Richard's plate, where his dinner turns from shepherd's pie to shepherd's soup.

"Oh no! I'm so sorry," Mom says.

"It wasn't your fault," Richard says, glaring at his son.

Ocean gazes wide-eyed at the table. But not like someone who's in trouble. More like someone who has discovered a new type of domino effect.

"Ocean!" Richard says.

"It's fine," Mom says.

"What?" Ocean asks.

"Apologize, please." The tops of Richard's cheeks are red again at the edge of his beard, but I think it's because he's mad, not because he's embarrassed. Or maybe he *is* embarrassed that he raised an alien instead of a child.

"Sorry," Ocean says, looking at Richard.

"Not to me!" Richard puts a hand to his head.

Ocean looks around, obviously bewildered.

"To Susan."

"Sorry, Susan," Ocean says.

Then Mom repeats that everything is fine, Richard gets up for a new plate of dinner, Ocean resumes patting his mashed potatoes with his fork, and I try again.

"So, my photos —"

"Richard, what do you think about going to the climate march?" Mom asks. "I'm working, but I could try to get free."

"You don't have to miss work. I can easily walk there with Simone," I say.

But no one hears me, because Ocean, while running his fork through his food, bursts out with sound effects from something called Tank Tour, a new game he's been playing with Jackson.

I silently count to ten. There is apparently research that says children who eat family dinners with their parents are better adjusted and become more successful adults. I'm 100 percent sure those researchers have never met Ocean.

We never get back to the climate march conversation. By the time we finish dinner, we're all holding our stomachs like overfed walruses. Except for Ocean, who has turned his plate into a war zone.

"You worked so hard," Mom tells Richard. "I'll do dishes."

She gives me a look.

"I'll help too," I say politely.

But Richard seems incapable of sharing his kitchen. And Ocean's incapable of playing by himself. This means all four of us are soon crammed into the townhouse kitchen. That's too many overfed walruses in one space. Plus, Richard's rearranging the dishes in the cupboards as quickly as I put them away.

After a few minutes, I leave my dish towel on the rack and step to the edge of the room, pretending to stretch. Quickly, Richard claims the towel. He puts Ocean in charge of drying the silverware. It's completely obvious there's no need for me here.

Before I leave, I remember one other thing we need to talk about. I have to do something about my school lunch issues. A vegan diet *is* good for the Earth. And Simone is getting more and more excited about this diet, because her mom found recipes for baking with avocados, and now Simone thinks brownies are a food group. (The brownies are shockingly good.)

"Do you ever make anything vegan?" I ask Richard.

"What's 'vegan'?" Ocean asks.

Richard snorts. "How do you know when someone's vegan?"

"How?"

"Don't worry. They'll tell you. Over and over again."

Mom giggles.

"I don't get it. What's 'vegan'?" Ocean asks.

His sentence is punctuated by a "cock-a-doodle-doo" as he opens Mom's ceramic rooster and snatches a cookie.

Ignoring both Ocean and the rooster, I try again. "Would it be hard to make my lunches vegan?"

"Emily, you love Richard's lunches," Mom says, pausing her pot-scrubbing.

Ocean has given up on sorting the spoons and started using them as percussion instruments. "Emily wants to be vegan. Emily wants to be vegan," he bangs out on a plastic container.

"It's not that," I say.

"You didn't like the shepherd's pie? I thought it was amazing," Mom says, drying her hands and wrapping an arm around Richard's waist. They both seem oblivious to Ocean's noise, which is reaching jet-engine levels.

"It was delicious. But there's this club at school that the new girl started. A vegan club. Daniella and Simone are already eating that way." Mom's known Simone for years, of course, and the one time she met Daniella, she talked for days about how sweet and polite Daniella was.

"Oh, honey," Mom says. "It's one thing to change how you eat because you feel strongly about something. But I didn't raise you to go along with the crowd."

"No, I can accommodate," Richard says. "It's important to fit in at that age."

"That's not —" I start, but no one's listening.

Richard gives my mom a squeeze. "You probably don't realize, because you were always one of the cool girls."

"I wasn't always a cool girl," she says, but it's obvious she's lying.

"Emily's a loser. Emily's a loser," Ocean drums.

"It's not to fit in," I protest again, but no one's listening.

"Emily's a loser. Emily's a loser."

"OCEAN!" I glare at him.

"Ocean, inside voice, please," Richard says. "And we don't call names."

"I still don't think it's reasonable to ask Richard to make you entirely separate lunches," Mom says.

"It's kind of related to climate action, and all the girls have joined this club, and —"

"Emily's a loser. Emily's a loser."

"OCEAN, SHUT UP!"

"EMILY!" Mom snaps.

And, of course, she's right. That was an inappropriate way to handle the situation. BUT THERE WERE REASONS!

"Ocean, time-out. In your room," Richard says.

Mom turns her attention to me. "That wasn't nice. Maybe you'd better take a few minutes to collect yourself."

I'm about to explain, in my most polite, reasonable manner. But then Ocean makes a face at me as he stomps out of the room. This leaves me with only two options. I can murder him (definitely impolite), or I can excuse myself.

I climb the stairs dejectedly. This was entirely NOT the way I intended the vegan conversation to end.

12

The Art of Betrayal

Simone promised to talk to Mr. Lau with me. She's supposed to be my moral support. But as soon as we arrive at school on Monday morning, Amelie snatches her away.

"I saw your YouHappy post about secondhand shops," Amelie says, without acknowledging my presence. "Have you been to Stolen Fancies? It's my absolute favorite."

Secondhand treasure hunting is one of our most fabulous talents. Before I can say that, though, Simone is gushing about how she desperately wants to go shopping with Amelie, and even though I'm basically jumping up and down in the background trying to remind her about saving the Earth, there's apparently nothing more important than vintage denim.

Then Amelie tucks her hair behind her ears and I see them. She's wearing the same long, sparkly earrings that Asha's been wearing on YouHappy! I searched for those earrings online, so I happen to know exactly how much they cost, which is approximately a billion times more than any eighth-grader is allowed to spend on accessories.

Simone hasn't even noticed the earrings yet. She's busy emoting over the shirt Amelie found at Stolen Fancies. As if Amelie needs to shop at secondhand stores.

That's it. I'm going to see the principal by myself.

They don't seem to notice when I leave, which irritates me enough to get me down the hall and all the way to the reception desk.

"Could I talk to Mr. Lau, please?"

We have two receptionists at Cedarview, both called Ms. Jennifer. This Ms. Jennifer wrinkles her nose.

"Oh, I don't know if he'll have time. Can I help you with something?"

"I really need to see Mr. Lau. I'll be quick," I promise.

"I'll ask if he can spare a minute," she says, as if she's requesting something special.

She gets up from the desk, straightens her skirt, and knocks quietly on the door. Mr. Lau barks from the other side, then Ms. Jennifer opens it a crack and has a whispered conversation.

Finally, I'm beckoned.

The chairs are pushed in tight against his desk, so I stand behind them.

"Emily," Mr. Lau says. "What can I do for you?"

I don't have time to answer before he's talking again. "I have a meeting this morning in just . . ." He checks his watch, "five minutes or so."

I take a deep breath. Thankfully I practiced my speech, so I can be extra efficient.

"Mr. Lau, I wrote a story for *Cedarview Speaks*, but Mr. Chadwick —"

"Great job on that September episode. Loved the part about using less paper and recycling juice boxes," he says.

"Thank you, but Mr. Chadwick said our story about the climate march was —"

"Now, I hope you're not too upset about one story. That's part of working on a creative project, isn't it? Taking constructive criticism? Developing a thick skin and all that?"

He gets up from his chair and starts for the door. Is he leaving?

I try to get my words out faster. "It's not that. The climate march is important and —"

"Of course it is. Of course it is. And I'm sure they'll do a great job of it. Here at Cedarview, though, our students are a little young to go traipsing unsupervised through the streets. And you have to consider your audience, don't you, when you're working on a project like this?"

He's not leaving. He's opening the door so *I* can leave.

"Well, I —"

"It's absolutely wonderful that you're taking this little podcast so seriously."

"It's not just a —"

"I agree. It's an excellent learning opportunity. Now, I have a meeting, but I'll look forward to hearing this month's episode."

I don't even realize my feet are moving until I find myself back in the reception area with Mr. Lau's door closed behind me. I stumble past the Ms. Jennifers and toward homeroom.

"Emily!" Simone finds me in the hallway partway there. "Are we going to talk to Mr. Lau?"

"I talked to him already."

"You did?" She grabs my elbow. "Were you fantabulous? What did he say?"

I look at her glumly. "I wasn't fantabulous, and he didn't change his mind."

"You should have waited for me!" she says. "Maybe two of us could have convinced him."

"I would have waited," I say, gritting my teeth. "But you were —"

That's when the bell rings, possibly saving our friendship.

As we walk from homeroom to math, Amelie rejoins us, still gushing about secondhand clothes. Apparently, she once found a vegan leather jacket for ten dollars.

We're about to slide into our desks when I spot Bryce heading toward Daniella's usual spot.

"Wait!" I say.

I guess I'm loud. The whole class turns to look at me.

"I really want to sit next to Daniella," I say.

Then I give a significant stare to Simone, hoping she'll realize why I'm rearranging the whole seating system.

She does. Because we're connected like that.

"I want to sit beside Daniella too," she says.

Amelie shrugs. "I guess I do too."

"Girls, we chose seats at the beginning of the year," Mr. Gill calls from the front of the room.

I turn my significant stare in his direction. "It's important that we change."

I don't know if my look works, or if he's just eager to start teaching. Mr. Gill throws his hands in the air. "Just sit somewhere, please, so we can get going."

The three of us arrange ourselves in a semicircle of desks around Daniella's front-row spot. She blushes a vivid shade of scarlet, but she mouths "Thank you" at me. Bryce ends up in the back row with Reza, which is his natural habitat anyway.

"So what do we do next?" Simone whispers once we're settled. "About Mr. Lau?"

I mostly forgive her for being insensitive earlier. "I do have a couple of ideas. I mentioned the march in my advice segment — we should record that after school. And we're going to make posters for Asha's visit, right? I thought we could add the climate march information."

"Fantabulous!" Simone says.

"Eyes up here," Mr. Gill calls.

"I'll bring some poster board to school," Simone whispers.

Posters. They seem only one step up from the climate change bulletin board that Mr. Chadwick suggested. As Mr. Gill rolls through the multiplication of fractions, I drum my fingers on the desk.

Posters are good. The advice column is good. But I'm not giving up on my real climate march story. Not yet.

I chase down Reza in the hallway between classes, which isn't easy. First, I have to duck a basketball pass from Bryce, then I almost breathe the backwash of some boy's burp. I should get hazard pay for being the producer of *Cedarview Speaks*.

"Reza, can we meet and record your podcast —"

I can't finish my question, because at the word "meet," the boys start hooting like wild hyenas.

I refuse to react. Interestingly, Reza's ears turn pink.

"Podcast. Recording." I make my words extra clear, so even hyenas can understand them.

"I can . . . um . . . record it. I can go to the studio before basketball."

"Or we can meet tomorrow morning," I say.

"Tomorrow morning," he repeats.

"Tomorrow," the hyenas repeat, as if we've made a date to . . . well, I don't even want to imagine what Reza and I would do on a date. Probably he'd bring along his basketball.

I leave the boys behind. As podcast producer, influencer, and future tour guide to Asha Jamil, I have much more important things to consider.

Simone comes through in record time. Her mom drops off poster-making supplies at lunch. We're going to put the climate march information in small letters, and we'll welcome Asha Jamil in big letters. That way, Mr. Lau won't notice the climate part. And since Asha's visit is the day before the march, Asha will pass the posters in the hallways and . . . eeep! She'll see the march info, and our level of initiative, and it will be the perfect spark for our conversation about social media influence and saving the Earth.

"My posters will be on the green poster board with a turquoise border, and yours will be on turquoise board with a green border," Simone says. "They'll be different enough to stand out, but they'll be super psychically linked in people's minds," she says. "That will double our brand recognition."

"Smart." She's going to be fabulous at marketing her fashion creations one day.

We claim Ms. Flores's classroom. Pushing aside some desks to create floor space, we spread out our materials.

"I'm going with an Earth-as-seen-from-space theme," I tell her, after a few minutes of consideration. "Climate march info at the bottom. Then I'll write '*Welcome, Asha Jamil*' at the top and decorate around the letters with yellow stars."

"Brilliant! And you should absolutotally do bubble letters."

I LOVE bubble letters, but mine always turn out like slightly deflated balloons.

"Can you sketch them for me?"

She does, and I'm so pleased with the results, I split my banana chocolate-chip muffin (Richard's latest masterpiece) and pass her half.

"Vegan?" she asks.

"Absolutely."

I have no idea, but it's not like there's meat hiding inside muffins, right?

Turning back to my poster, I carefully sketch star shapes around the words, then start coloring them. I think I'm going to cut out some construction paper stars, too, and glue them so they extend past the edges.

"I haven't figured out my slogan yet," Simone says, staring at her own poster board. "I need something super amazing. Something splendiferous."

"*Welcome to Our Splendiferous Star*."

She shakes her head. "Too long."

"*Asha Jamil, You're Our Star.*"

A noncommittal sound.

"Give me some ideas, and we'll work from there," I tell her.

"It's hard to alliterate properly with 'Jamil.'" She sighs.

I'm sure there's a solution. In fact, I'm probably on the cusp of a spectacular brain wave when a swath of strawberry blond hair floats into the doorway.

"What are you doing?" Amelie asks.

Why, why, why didn't we shut the door? What kind of top-secret poster campaign happens with the door wide open?

"We're making posters to welcome Asha."

"Oh, I wanted to do posters too, for the vegan club."

Amelie continues to stand in the doorway, smiling. I smile half-heartedly back, waiting for her to leave. But then . . .

"Why don't you join us? I'm completely, seriously stuck for a slogan," Simone says.

I almost spit out my last bite of muffin. And before I can spit out a genius solution that will totally negate the need for outside help, Amelie is perched on the floor between us. Simone gives her the overview of our semi-matching posters, my wording, and her own lack of alliterative options.

"Wow, you're so organized. My mom didn't have time to get me paper board for my vegan club posters. Her work has been super busy," she says.

"Why don't you grab a piece of ours? We have lots," Simone offers.

I stare at my best friend, who's known me for years, who would never betray me. I *need* to stare because it seems

A LOT like she's offering Amelie a chance to share our color scheme and use it for completely different purposes. And yes, she's handing over a sheet of turquoise. *My* turquoise.

"This is so nice of you. Thanks," Amelie says.

This may look like muffin crumbs. It's actually my brain, which exploded on the classroom floor!

Simone gasps, and for a moment I think she too might have had an aneurysm. Then she says, "Amelie, what if Asha endorsed your vegan campaign?!"

"But..."

That's all I manage. I can't really say, "But *I'm* the one who's supposed to meet Asha."

It's as if we're back at the lunch table and I have chicken stuck in my throat again. Maybe a whole chicken this time, with feathers.

Neither of them pays attention to me.

"Someone with her influence could really spread the word about plant-based eating," Simone says.

"So true!" Amelie says.

"We have extra markers, too," Simone says.

And before the traitorous dagger can sink fully into my heart, Amelie is sketching her very own turquoise and green poster, right in the middle of our workspace.

She stops suddenly and puts down her marker. I have a brief flare of hope. Maybe she's realized that using our poster board is the worst idea ever.

"What am I doing? I can't start yet. We need to find you a slogan!" she says to Simone.

"*Asha Jamil, You're Our Star,*" I say flatly.

"It's a bit dull," Amelie says.

There's a pause while Simone and Amelie look to the sky for ideas.

"What about *Asha, Our Superstar*, and a picture of Asha wearing a cape?"

Simone applauds. She actually applauds.

"It's perfect!" She turns to me. "Isn't it supremely perfect?"

"Supremely. You could cut out the cape so it looks like it's flying off the page," I say. Because she may as well take all the best ideas at once.

She nods happily and starts to sketch.

After a while, I forgive her. The whole reason she's my best friend is because she's sweet and generous. It's not her fault her generosity is misdirected at the moment.

Making my new posters pop with the help of my bestie @SustainableSimone.

I take a picture of the top of my poster where it overlaps with Simone's. Then I crop it perfectly, so Amelie's work doesn't distract from the theme.

Asha will probably be amazed at our climate-action commitment. She'll probably take her own photos of our posters and add them to her YouHappy feed. And then, if she tags us . . .

I'm picturing the scene so intently, I barely hear the squeak of markers, the rustling of paper, or any alliteration whatsoever. Until Simone touches me on the shoulder.

"Emily? The bell's going to ring soon."

I look around to find that she's finished one of her posters. Because she's a much, much better artist than I am, Asha's cape flows perfectly off the edge of her paper.

Amelie, on her first attempt, has drawn THE ART OF LIFE, in block letters, surrounded by vines, bees, and flowers. In smaller letters at the bottom, it says *Eat a Plant-Based Diet and Save Our Planet!* It's possibly the most beautiful poster I've ever seen.

"You didn't get much done," she says, looking at my half-colored attempt. "Are those supposed to be stars?"

"No." Well, yes, but there's no need for her to mock my artistic abilities. It was hard to get the yellow to show up on the turquoise background.

"We can give you a hand, later today. Now that we're all in this together," she says.

Simone nods so enthusiastically, her bob bounces.

I force myself to smile. "That's all right. I'm busy after school, so I'll work on these at home tonight. I've got plenty of time."

In fact, I'll have plenty of time for the rest of my middle-grade career because my best friend has been distracted by shiny, vegan things. As we're dividing up the art supplies for the evening, I make sure to grab the magenta marker and the black fine-liner. If I lose the chance to meet Asha *and* wind up friendless, it won't be because of faulty art supplies.

I'm heading for class when I see a flash of red hair.

"Daniella?"

She scurries around the corner, but I chase after her. When I catch up, I can tell she's been crying. Her cheeks are even more flushed than usual.

"What's going on?"

She swipes at her eyes. "It's just Bryce."

I have a sudden realization. "We left you all by yourself in the cafeteria at lunch. We were making posters. I'm so sorry."

"It's fine. I have to figure it out. My dad wants me to take karate."

"Seriously?" I try to imagine Daniella karate-chopping Bryce to the cafeteria floor. It's definitely a satisfying image . . . but maybe not realistic. "He thinks you can fight Bryce?"

"He wants me to be more assertive."

"Well . . . it might be sort of fun. My pseudo-brother goes, and he —"

"I signed up for a computer course instead," she says.

Which is not going to help with the bullying situation, but I guess if it makes her happy, that's okay?

The bell rings.

"We should get to class," I say.

"You go ahead. I have a stomach-ache. I think I'll go home for the afternoon."

I watch her walk away, then I head to social studies, feeling like I have a stomach-ache of my own. Maybe I should have offered to join karate with her. Maybe I should have offered to karate-chop Bryce myself.

"You okay?" I text her, an hour later.

"Just busy."

That's all I get before science class starts, forcing me to tuck my cell away. Ms. Flores is known for confiscating phones and calling parents. That's the last thing I need.

13

Things Get Gassy

Simone holds up Mr. Chadwick's favorite new possession.

"Testing the mic. Testing our fabulous mic."

On the screen in front of her, squiggles appear, like miniature heartbeats. I pop in an earbud and listen to the playback. Sounds good!

Simone misses my thumbs-up gesture because she's busy making weird sounds and watching more squiggles appear.

"Ready?" I ask, once her alien noises stop.

"Ready."

It was hard to get out of bed early this morning, but now that Simone and I are ensconced in the podcast studio, I feel like we're in an ideal world. The two of us, plus all the equipment we need to influence the universe. Or at least the school.

"Hey! Sorry I'm late!"

Make that the *three* of us. Reza bursts into the studio smelling . . . well, actually he smells surprisingly good for once. Like he might have discovered deodorant.

"Sorry. Were you recording?" he whispers.

"Just about to start." I wave him toward the third chair, then I press record.

"What's next in our episode, Simone?"

I remember to smile as I talk. Apparently, people can hear smiles. That was in one of the first podcasting tutorials we watched with Mr. Chadwick.

"Well, Emily . . ."

It doesn't take long to record our piece, because Simone and I achieve near-flawless excellence on our first try, even with Reza watching, listening, and making bunny ears behind Simone. We leave the audio files for Daniella's final edit, then Reza takes over at the microphone.

"Need help?" I offer. Because I'm an excellent producer.

"I got this. But it's okay if you stay," he says.

Simone tugs my sleeve. "If we have ten minutes before the bell, should we hang posters?"

And that completes the perfect Tuesday morning! Abandoning Reza, we borrow tape from Mr. Chadwick's desk and decorate the hallways with our posters of perfection. Everything's happening according to plan.

Then Simone ruins it.

"I'm so glad we got this done," she says.

The hallways are bustling now, as everyone heads for homeroom.

"I know! We are so productive."

"Efficient-anado." She nods. "I promised Amelie I'd help hang her posters at lunch hour, and I wasn't sure when I was going to have time to do yours."

My feet stop.

Someone steps on my heel. I spin to find Reza directly behind me.

"Are you done already?"

He raises his hands in the air, like I'm the hallway police. "Sorry! I wanted to tell you it's exactly three minutes long, like you said. And the audio files are on the computer."

"Thank you," I say, using all my politeness skills. Hopefully three minutes of basketball won't make the entire school stop listening to the podcast.

When I turn back to confront Simone about scheduling Amelie's poster-hanging before checking with me about my poster-hanging needs, she's doing fake European cheek kisses with Amelie.

"Gross," Reza says.

This is the first time we've ever agreed on something.

"They are pure fabulosity," Simone gushes. I imagine she's talking about Amelie's posters, which Amelie's now sliding back into a cardboard poster roll. Because of course Amelie has the perfect container for her perfect posters.

Reza taps my shoulder. "So, do you want to listen to my podcast —"

"Not now!"

He takes a step back.

I didn't mean to say it quite so loudly.

"Sorry. I don't have time now. But I'm sure you did it perfectly." My second try is significantly better. But I can't help a small foot stomp on my way into homeroom.

I don't speak to Simone at any point in our morning classes — not that she notices. And fortunately, I'm the only one at the lunch table, so I can practice my confident independence and eat my shepherd's pie in peace. It's not exactly pleasant eating by myself. But there's something about Richard's food that makes me feel a tiny iota better.

I stop at my locker and drop off my thermos. I sit through a perfectly uneventful social studies class. By the time I get to science, I'm beginning to think it's possible that I overreacted this morning. Maybe.

Ms. Flores smiles at me. "Emily! Just the person I need."

It's nice to be appreciated and recognized for my dedication to school.

"Can you run the attendance folder to the office? I forgot to send it down earlier."

Okay, while that's not exactly what I expected, it's good to know that Ms. Flores relies on me. I take the folder from her hands and hurry toward the office. But when I turn the corner toward the stairs, I almost slam right into Daniella and Amelie. They're carrying a large cardboard box between them.

"Breakable!" Amelie calls.

"What are you doing?"

"Ms. Flores needed the beakers out of the storage room," Daniella whispers.

"She gave us her keys," Amelie says. "She said these are really fragile, so we were the only ones she'd trust."

"Daniella, are you feeling better?"

"She's fine," Amelie says. "Bryce issues. We already talked about it. She has a plan now."

"Computer science?" I ask doubtfully.

"She told you? Great," Amelie says. "I'm *so* excited about this."

I open my mouth and close it again, like the library goldfish.

"These things are heavy," Amelie says.

I step aside so they can whisk their precious cargo through. Then I stomp toward the office with my folder in hand. My completely unbreakable folder that doesn't require any special keys at all.

I'm being silly, I tell myself. This is petty. Daniella and Amelie were probably the first ones in the classroom, and it was pure, random chance that they were the ones asked to retrieve the beakers. Of course they'd talk while they worked. It's nice that Amelie's supporting Daniella's interests, even if those interests aren't useful.

But it seems like every five minutes, by pure random chance, Amelie's doing something ANNOYING.

I leave the folder on Ms. Jennifer's desk and start back toward class. I pass a few of Simone's posters on the way, and a few of mine. But Amelie's posters are everywhere. About half of them say *Join Amelie C. — Save the Earth and Sea!* There are tiny pictures of compost bins and recycling signs and garden boxes . . . all things that Amelie wants to add to the school. I wouldn't have thought compost bins could be attractive, but they somehow are. The other half of her posters say, *THE ART OF LIFE. Join the Vegan Club Today!* They're decorated with swirling flowers, leaves, and bees.

As I reach the top of the stairs, I happen to have my hand in the pocket of my hoodie. And in that pocket, I happen to have the black fine-liner pen I stuffed in there when we made the posters.

I glance back and forth, up and down the stairs. There's no one coming.

And then, before I can even think the words "moral values" or "a responsible person would never do this," I pull out the pen and uncap it.

Three little black lines.

That's all it takes to turn THE ART OF LIFE into THE FART OF LIFE.

For a moment, those three little black lines make me ridiculously happy. I maybe even giggle to myself in the hallway. I feel so much better about the beakers, my lack of social media presence, my inability to eat shepherd's pie without feeling guilty . . .

Then I hear a soft whistle.

My heart stops. I swear, it literally stops. And I cap the pen and shove it into my pocket faster than I've ever done anything in my life.

Eighth-grader found unconscious in school hallway. Foul play suspected.

Maybe because I'm having a cardiac incident, it takes me a minute to find the source of the whistle. It's Marcus, sitting by himself behind a study carrel in the hallway.

"Marcus, what are you —"

Before I finish my sentence, he's up and hurrying away from me down the hall, his lab coat flapping behind him.

When I get back to class, my heart's still pounding in my chest. Did he see me draw on the poster? He must have. Will he tell?

"Thank you, Emily. There's a free workstation beside Reza, and you can start your experiment," Ms. Flores calls.

Reza explains the assignment in surprisingly normal sentences, for a boy.

"You have a beaker and three unknown liquid substances," he says. "You're supposed to mix the substances and record your observations."

"Thanks."

It's perfectly obvious that the liquids are vinegar, oil, and water.

"*Substance A has a harsh, sour smell,*" I write.

I am not someone who defaces other people's posters. What was I thinking?

"*Substance B does not mix with Substance C.*"

"You have nice handwriting," Reza says.

"Thanks."

He's been shockingly normal today. Maybe even for more than one day. But I have no time to ponder Reza's mental development. Because what if Marcus tells on me? I'll be so humiliated, I'll never be able to show my face at school again. I'll have to transfer. Probably to Inuvik. Hopefully they don't have internet that far north, and no one will hear of my criminal past.

"*Substance C has no notable smell.*"

Unlike me. I smell like guilt. Insurmountable guilt.

The PA system crackles to life. "Please excuse this interruption. Will Emily Laurence report to the office? Emily Laurence."

Crash! My beaker shatters on the science room floor, coating everything with a shiny layer of Substance B and the smell of imminent doom.

"Goodness, Emily!" Ms. Flores says.

"I'll get paper towels," Reza says.

"No. Step back. There are shards of glass. Reza, run for the custodian. Emily, you'd better head for the office."

I stop by Ms. Flores's desk on the way out of the classroom. "I'm really sorry," I tell her. "And if I don't come back, I want you to know that you're an amazing science teacher."

She looks confused. "That's very kind, Emily, but I'm sure you'll be right back. Hurry up and see what Mr. Lau needs."

The walk to the office feels like a trip across the Sahara. Or up Mount Everest, except that I have to climb *down* all the stairs and directly past the evidence of my criminal act. The whole way, I try to think of a reasonable explanation. The whole way, I fail.

Her criminal career began in childhood. Read the sordid story here.

I'll be the star of one of those trashy news sites that give you a computer virus as soon as you click on them.

Emily Post once wrote that cowardly lies are the blackest of black lies.

The blackest of black.

But I didn't really lie. It's not as if anyone asked about the posters.

At that thought, my stomach clenches. What if someone *does* ask?

By the time I reach Mr. Lau's desk, my whole body's sweating.

He doesn't seem to notice. "We've lost Marcus again. Rob is already searching for him, but I'm swamped here."

When is he going to get to the part about vandalism?

He stops typing and glances up at me. "You and Marcus seem to have a bit of a bond. Could you help with the search?"

I stare. I was so busy bracing for my prison sentence, I've barely absorbed his words.

"Is that okay? Sorry to pull you out of class."

"NO, that's FINE!"

My voice comes out extra loudly, and I have to try again.

"That's fine. Of course, I'll help look for him."

"You're a lifesaver," he says.

Which is obviously not true, but he has already turned back to his screen.

Marcus isn't in the library, the upstairs bathroom, behind the kiln in the art room, or in any of the other dozen places I look for him. Every few minutes, I pass Rob in the hallway. He looks more and more stressed. His hair keeps sticking up farther from his head. If we don't find Marcus soon, it might fly right off his scalp.

I stop searching random places and stand in the middle of the downstairs hallway, thinking hard. Where would I hide if I were sick of this school?

I'm staring at the wall as I think. Slowly, one of the posters comes into focus. One of Amelie's "Art of Life" posters. Except it doesn't say THE ART OF LIFE. It says THE FART OF LIFE.

And this is not the poster I changed.

I walk a few steps down the hall until I find another one. FART OF LIFE.

The next. *FART OF LIFE.*

Each one is defaced in a different color.

Just as I'm beginning to realize the true horribleness of this situation, Rob appears at the other end of the hallway. Marcus trails behind him, hands stuffed in the pockets of his lab coat.

"Found him!" Rob calls. "Thanks for your help, Emily!"

A streak of marker stretches from the collar to the pocket of Marcus's lab coat.

He winks as Rob hurries him past me. "I finished them for you."

I stand there with my mouth hanging open.

"We'll make a stop at the office, bud, and have a little chat about vandalism," Rob is saying.

I trail after them. One of the Ms. Jennifers pops up from behind her desk. "Why don't you head straight into Mr. Lau's office?"

I watch them disappear. Then I stand by the reception desk for a little while, taking one step toward Mr. Lau's door and one step away, again and again. No one calls my name. No shouting erupts. The whole school seems silent.

I should really tell Mr. Lau about the posters.

But maybe this is the best thing that could happen to my campaign to meet Asha. It may not be exactly fair, but I'm not the one who defaced all the posters. And it's certainly convenient. Everyone will be laughing at Amelie's vegan club. There's no way she'll be chosen to meet Asha.

And really, isn't this the best result for everyone? I have no doubt I'm the ideal person to offer a school tour.

"Did you need something, sweetheart?"

The other Ms. Jennifer bustles in, a pile of papers in her arms.

Do I need something?

"Um . . . I just wanted to make sure Marcus is okay?"

"Aren't you an angel? I'm sure Rob has called his mom. He'll be just fine."

"Right . . . angel," I say, nodding.

Slowly, I turn back toward class, leaving my moral compass somewhere behind me on the office floor.

14

Eavesdropping Etiquette

As Amelie peels the lid from her quinoa salad at lunch, Simone sighs.

"I still want to be part of the vegan club, but the only choices today are cheeseburgers and chicken fingers," she says.

Daniella wrinkles her nose, examining Simone's plate. "You could peel off the meat and eat the bun," she whispers.

"But it might have eggs."

"Plus you'd be wasting a lot of food," I say. Because it's obvious that Simone actually wants to eat her cheeseburger, which has been her favorite cafeteria lunch since forever, something she may have forgotten when she embarked on this vegan enterprise.

Daniella opens her lunchbox to reveal sliced carrots cut in flower shapes, cucumber curlicues, and tiny sticky-rice balls dotted with sesame seeds.

"Wow," Simone says. "Your mom really loves you."

"I make my own lunches," Daniella says, but no one hears her except me, and I have bigger issues to think about.

I turn to Amelie. "I saw what happened to your posters."

She groans. "I know! Mr. Lau called me in to explain, and then some guy named Rob helped me take them all down."

My stomach feels like a compost bin.

"Completely tragical!" Simone says.

Amelie sighs. "I guess I'll make some more. I feel kind of bad for that Marcus kid, too. He was still sitting in the office when I left."

That settles it. I'm the absolute worst.

Simone suddenly throws her hands in the air. "Maybe we can interview you on the podcast. About the vegan club!"

"Really?" Amelie and I say it at the same time. In not quite the same way.

"We'll help get the word out," Simone says. "And you'll be great in an interview."

Amelie claps her hands. "That would be amazing! You are seriously the most supportive people I've ever met. I'm so lucky to have found you."

And now someone has lit my internal compost bin on fire.

"Oh, but you two will have to fix your posters, too. Right?" Amelie says, looking suddenly concerned.

Simone and I glance at one another. "Why?"

"Because Asha's tour dates have changed. She's going to be here next Friday. I heard Mr. Lau telling one of the teachers."

"Next Friday!" Simone and I gasp the words simultaneously.

"That's the climate —"

"What have we been thinking?" Simone interrupts me.
"We need to plan our outfits!"
"I know!" Amelie says. "I'm going to trim my bangs after school this afternoon. Do you want me to do yours, Simone? I could come to your house."
"What about the climate —"
But I get interrupted again.
"Are you really going to eat that?" Amelie asks Simone, manga eyes wide. She puts her hand on Simone's arm.
Simone's cheeseburger hovers in the air.
"Um..."
I put Asha's visit to one side of my brain for a tiny nanosecond.
"She has to eat it, or she'll starve for the rest of the afternoon," I say.
Simone flashes me a grateful look.
"Maybe she can become a vegan gradually, over time?" Daniella whispers.
Amelie is busy fuming about factory farming, whatever that is. "And one cow can release 70 to 120 kilograms of methane per year, unless it's grass-fed, and I highly doubt this cafeteria is springing for grass-fed beef. Who runs this place, anyway?"
She looks around, as if expecting a butler to appear.
"Ms. Lydia," Simone, Daniella, and I chorus, in the same ominous tone.
We glance to the corner where she usually stations herself. She wears her gray hair scraped back in a bun so tight it stretches the skin at her temples. Rumor has it Ms. Lydia was last seen smiling more than a decade ago.

"Well," Amelie says, pushing back her chair, "she and I are going to have a little talk."

And with that, she stalks off to change the world.

Simone takes an enormous bite of her cheeseburger.

"*Ust for toway*," she says with her mouth full. "*Towally wegan tomowwow*."

I glance around cautiously. Until now, I've only been eating my grapes. But Amelie has indeed found Ms. Lydia, and the two of them appear to be deep in conversation. I quickly unwrap my sandwich. It's brie and pear, which sounds strange but is the most delicious thing ever. It's one of my favorite Richard creations, and even though it's not vegan, it's at least vegetarian.

I tear off one corner and pass it to Simone, who stuffs it in her mouth and mini-swoons between frantic cheeseburger bites.

Over by the lunch counter, Amelie's voice is rising.

"Twenty-first century . . . diversity of students . . . whole foods . . . processed dreck!"

I can't hear Ms. Lydia. Is it possible she looks even more pinched than usual? She's a big fan of proper mealtime behavior. She once complimented me on the way I hold my cutlery. She and Emily Post would probably be besties. I can't wait until she loses her patience, gives Amelie her patented death glare, and then . . .

". . . principal's office," Ms. Lydia says, pointing to the cafeteria door.

Wow, she skipped all the in-between stages and went straight to the office-point.

I knew this would happen! At least, once Amelie's gone, Simone and I can talk properly about Asha's visit.

Bryce struts by our table just then. He reaches over, grabs one of Daniella's carrot flowers, and pops it in his mouth. Without asking!

All three of us glare as he walks away.

"That . . . that . . . Neanderthalatus!" Simone spits.

Daniella just looks tired.

Then we're distracted by Amelie, who hustles back to our table to grab her stuff. She'll probably have to eat lunch in the office for the rest of the week.

"We should have warned you about Ms. Lydia," I say.

"You totally should have! I had no idea she has such a history of digestive problems," Amelie says.

This is a strange way to put things.

"As soon as the bell rings, she's going to meet me in the office to discuss plant-based menus with Mr. Lau. I hope we can at least do meatless Mondays."

I am so speechless, I forget that language exists.

"I have to grab some resources from my locker. I think I have a book about the industrial food complex."

As she turns to leave, she glances back at us. "Thanks, everyone. This wouldn't have happened without the vegan club!"

I've already shoved the cover onto my sandwich remnants. Simone's holding her last cheeseburger bite behind her back.

"See you later this afternoon!"

"*This abternoon*," Simone agrees. Apparently she's still chewing.

Then Amelie's gone.

"What's the industrial food complex?" Daniella whispers. I have no idea, and no one else heard her question.

Before lunch ends, I set off to find Mr. Lau and make sure Amelie was right about the date change. But neither of the Ms. Jennifers is in the reception area. I stand there uncertainly, trying to decide whether to poke my head into Mr. Lau's office. His door is open slightly. I could knock?

Then I hear his voice. He's talking on the phone.

"That climate march nonsense?" he says.

Emily Post is firmly against eavesdropping. And if Mr. Lau had said any words other than "climate march," I would have spun around and scuttled directly to class. But instead I stand frozen by the reception desk.

"No, we don't have a problem here," he says. "I understand what you mean, about the school board needing to set a policy, but it's not going to be an issue on our end."

A pause.

"Right. I've got some sort of fashion icon visiting that day. The girls are all starry-eyed. They won't be going anywhere. You know it's always the girls who lead these things."

I can't even breathe. Is he really saying what I think he's saying?

A teacher walks by, and I hold my breath until the clicking of her high heels has faded away toward the staff room. She doesn't notice me.

"I know. It was a happy coincidence." Mr. Lau's voice echoes. "Sara, our social studies teacher, saw this opportunity to invite the Jamil woman, and I was able to reschedule her for next Friday."

Yes. He's saying exactly what I think he's saying.

"Drum up a few more Jamils?" He belly-laughs. "I'll do my best for you."

There's another long pause. It's time to back away. But I'm so angry, part of me wants to march directly into the office and accuse Mr. Lau of . . . climate sabotage!

"I hear you. Let's circle back to this in a couple of days," he says.

Before I can even think about what to do next, he appears in his office doorway. For a brief moment, when he's still looking at his phone, I think maybe I can escape. Then he looks up.

Our eyes meet. His eyebrows arch. He glances down at his phone, then back at me. His mouth presses into a grim line.

I should pretend to be surprised to see him. I should pretend to be someone who just this moment happened to wander into the office foyer and who would never, ever eavesdrop on a principal's private phone conversation. But I can't seem to control my horrified, mortally betrayed face.

"Emily," he says. "Why aren't you having lunch with your pals?"

I search frantically for an excuse. And suddenly, magically, Marcus appears beside me. He seems to have crawled out from underneath the reception desk. He brushes off his pants as if this is the world's most normal situation.

"She was looking for me," he says.

"Marcus, I —"

I don't want him to get in trouble. But he does provide the perfect excuse.

Mr. Lau pinches the bridge of his nose. "Marcus, I thought your mom was picking you up?"

"Not here yet."

"And where's Rob?"

"I can't keep track of him." Marcus sighs.

Mr. Lau stares at both of us for a minute. Then he shakes his head.

"Marcus, you wait here. On a chair," he adds firmly.

Then he looks at me and points toward the hallway. "Off to class. Bell's going to ring soon, and you don't want to be late."

He drops his phone into his suit pocket and turns back toward his desk.

Marcus drops into a chair. "I guess that's one more escape pod compromised." He sighs, shaking his head.

"Thanks for covering for me," I say.

He says something else about hiding spots, but I'm barely listening as I leave the reception area. All I can hear is Mr. Lau's last word. *Late, late, late.*

It seems to echo from the cinder block walls. *Late, late, late.*

Asha Jamil is being used to keep kids from the climate march. Everything's arranged. Am I too late to do anything?

15

Organized Crime

I feel sick. Not cold-or-flu sick. No, I feel sick about my own criminal tendencies. I thought I was someone who valued rules and etiquette and kindness. Then I defaced Amelie's poster and inspired Marcus to commit serious vandalism. What if poster defacing is a gateway drug, and he launches into a life of crime?

I think I'm about to do something worse, too. I think I'm about to stage a podcast coup.

A long time ago, when I was having nightmares as a little kid, Mom took me to a counselor named Ms. Minty. Her name sounded like peppermint, and she smelled like peppermint, too. According to Ms. Minty, some people are born with more alert nervous systems. She said I should learn to recognize what stress felt like inside my body. And when I felt that stress, I could choose — with my brain — how I wanted to react.

Easy for her to say. She had a calm, perfectly quiet office filled with stuffed animals.

But it doesn't take a psychology degree to figure out that wrecking Amelie's posters wasn't the best way to deal with stress. Also, it's possible I'm still mad at Mr. Chadwick. And furious at Mr. Lau.

Girl psychoanalyzes herself so accurately, experts are amazed.

When school's finally over, I wait at my locker for Simone. The hallways slowly empty. I linger for ten minutes before I remember the haircut plans; she isn't here to help. This also means she isn't here to change my mind.

I head for the library, arriving as Mr. Chadwick flicks off the lights.

"Could I stay for a few minutes?" I beg. "I need to record my replacement piece for this week's episode and do a bit of editing. I'll make sure to lock the door after."

I probably could have said half as many words. He's nodding before I finish, turning the lights back on. Then I'm alone in the ink-scented silence of the library.

I let myself into the podcast studio, turn on the computer and the mixer, and settle in front of the microphone. I feel almost like a spy, about to send a coded message. Except there's no code.

Set up. Audio test. Record.

"*Hello! I'm Emily Laurence. Welcome to* Cedarview Speaks."

Deep breath. Swallow.

"*Thanks for tuning in to this bonus episode. Our official October episode doesn't go live until next week, but I wanted you to learn about an upcoming climate march. I have an extra-special interview for you, with one of the organizers.*"

This is where I'll splice in my recordings of Mya. Then I'll need a few wrap-up sentences.

"*Climateers leader Mya Parsons says climate change is the biggest crisis humanity has ever faced. She encourages everyone to speak up. Together, we can demand more action from corporations and from the government.*

"*Hope to see you at the climate march on Friday, October 29!*"

Now for the editing. Daniella's job is harder than it looks, but eventually I get the clips smooshed together. I listen to everything one more time. It's not perfect, but the message is there. I save the file and stare at it for a little while. Am I really going to do this?

A noise in the library startles me and I leap from my chair and peek out the door, but it's only the custodian stacking the chairs.

No more waiting. No more worrying. Turning back to the computer, I click the button and watch the bar scroll all the way through. Bonus episode officially published. It's uploaded to the school website, and all our subscribers will get a notice that our newest episode is available.

I turn off the equipment.

It's the custodian's turn to startle as I emerge from the studio. He quickly smiles and waves, because he has no idea I'm a hardened criminal. I feel as if Persephone knows. She stares at me, aghast, from the other side of the fish tank glass.

I shrug at her. It's done. And even though I'm going to be in more trouble than ever before in my entire life, I actually feel better. I feel like I've done the right thing.

Maybe Emily Post wouldn't be too shocked. She once said: "Etiquette must, if it is to be of more than trifling use, include ethics as well as manners. Certainly what one is, is of far greater importance than what one appears to be."

What I *am* is a delinquent. But for excellent ethical reasons.

My moral conviction lasts until dinnertime. Then I panic. I can barely swallow Richard's fried rice.

"Did you hand-make these dumplings?" Mom asks.

Richard's cheeks turn pink. "Doesn't take too long."

I know he's been making them since before I arrived home from school, but that knowledge is somewhere in a different, still-functioning part of my brain. The part that notices Ocean coating his fried rice in ketchup. The part that manages to chew, swallow, and occasionally nod. The small part that isn't pulsing with red and blue alarm lights.

I'm in so much trouble.

The thing is, I could confess. I could tell Mom and Richard what I've done, and they could call the school, and they might even manage to make things okay. But somewhere in that process, my bonus episode would be deleted. And I would lose the imaginary argument I've been having with Mr. Lau and Mr. Chadwick in my head. I hate losing.

Once the dishes are done and I'm back in the safety of my room, I sink onto my purple rug and check my phone. There are a dozen messages from Simone.

Your podcast piece! What is happening???

Did Mr. Chadwick change his mind?

OMG. You went rogue, didn't you?

WHY AREN'T YOU TEXTING ME?

I get my hair cut on ONE AFTERNOON and you mutiny. WITHOUT ME!

I feel so left out.

Also, when you get suspended, I'll totally bring your homework to you.

Do you think you'll get suspended?

Sorry, not helpful.

WHY AREN'T YOU TEXTING ME???

I call her. She picks up the phone before it even rings.
"I can't believe you did that!"
"Me neither." I'm a strange mix of exhilarated and nauseated.
"What do you think they're going to do? Will they notice, do you think? Do you think you're going to get in serious trouble? What made you do this?"
Why do all of Simone's questions require so much thinking?
I try to explain. "I'm still mad that we aren't allowed to talk about something important. Especially when Mya's working so hard to organize the march."
"I am entirely impressed."

It makes me feel a little better, knowing she agrees with me. And I figure I may as well get my other criminal acts off my chest. At least, some of them.

"You know the selfie I posted last week?" I whisper, with a glance at my closed bedroom door. "My mom still doesn't know."

"You did that without asking?" She immediately grasps the seismic importance of this.

"It was kind of an accident."

I explain what happened in the library. But then I tell her to check my YouHappy feed. There are now five selfies, including one of me with my school poster, in which I've tagged @realAshaJamil, and —

I put Simone on speaker so I can scroll properly.

"Oh, I almost forgot I posted that one!"

It's a picture of one of the juice-box recycling bins. I've captioned it:

My BFF made these. Every little bit helps!

Simone squeals. "How did I not notice this?"

"Probably because my feed is usually so boring."

"You're up to fifty followers!"

I look again. FIFTY FOLLOWERS! One is an army sergeant named PowerPatty9430845, with no posts and no followers, and one is a shirtless man selling essential oils. I block them. But that's still A LOT more people being influenced by ME.

"This is how it begins," Simone says. "Next stop, red carpet."

"Unless my mom finds out."

Simone snorts. "Eventually, your mom will see how you're using your account for the good of the world," she says. "How could she possibly object?"

She's right. I feel so much better.

Simone will probably have helpful insights about the whole Marcus/posters/vandalism situation, too. I consider telling her that story, but she starts raving about the vegan hair products Amelie recommends. Then I start thinking about how perfect Amelie's hair is, and how imperfect mine is. The urge to discuss the posters temporarily disappears.

I'm sure it will come back. I just need the right moment.

While Simone blathers away on speaker, I scroll through my phone and find an old photo of the two of us. Her straight dark hair against my frizz . . . which almost looks like real curls in the sunlight.

A best friend makes everything better. Let's change the world together! #BFFs

It's not just an imaginary caption. I actually post the picture on YouHappy.

And Simone immediately hearts my post!

I know that the like buttons on social media channels are responsible for tiny doses of happy-chemicals inside the brain, and those doses can get addictive. But at this exact moment, I don't care, because, in the words of my best-ever friend, it's fabulatastic!

When my bedroom door swings open, I almost have a heart attack. I click back to my home screen faster than anyone has ever clicked in the history of technology.

"Emily, put your phone away, please," Mom says, dropping a pile of laundry on the end of my bed. "Get some sleep."

"Simone, I have to go."

"Good night to my favorite crimi —"

I hang up quickly.

"Crimini mushroom," I blurt, as Mom raises her eyebrows. "We have new fungus nicknames."

She leaves my room, shaking her head. When she peeks in a few minutes later, I've managed to move my laundry to the chair and I've climbed under my covers. Thanks to Simone's support, I've resisted pulling them over my head. I think things are going to be okay. I just need to figure out how to explain everything to Mr. Chadwick and convince him that I was right.

"Sweet dreams, love," Mom says.

But I lie awake for a long time, a dozen different strategies swirling in my head.

16

Wing Nuts

I wake up bleary-eyed and headachy on Wednesday. I walk to school slowly through soggy streets, wondering if it's possible I could be sucked into a different dimension. Or maybe an earthquake could strike the school at this exact moment, and the whole building could be declared unfit for human use.

As I reach the main doors, a car door slams behind me. "Thanks, Dad!"

It's Daniella's voice. I glance back to see a sleek black car pulling away from the curb. I only catch a quick glimpse, but the driver looks slightly familiar.

Daniella rushes toward me. "Ugh, this rain. I think we'd better hurry, or we're going to be late."

She seems normal as I hold the door and she scoots through. She doesn't mention the podcast.

Maybe no one except Simone bothered to listen. Maybe Mr. Chadwick and Mr. Lau didn't even notice the new episode.

Daniella glances over her shoulder. "How did you convince Mr. Chadwick?"

Okay, so everyone knows.

If only I had an answer to her question.

"Um . . . you're right. We're going to be late."

But she puts her hand on my arm.

"Emily . . . I want to say that . . . well, even though my dad . . . I'm personally really proud that . . ."

I don't figure out what she's talking about before we reach the classroom. We barely slide into our desks before the bell — I'm still wearing my wet coat.

"Living on the edge this morning?" Ms. Flores asks wryly, with a glance at the clock.

She has no idea.

I ignore the first half of the announcements as I struggle out of my coat and attempt to organize my books for the morning. Then I hear the word "star" and my head pops up.

Principal Lau has taken over the announcements.

". . . earned acclaim for her thoughtful portrayals of various women of color, bringing them to life on the screen."

"What's he talking about?" I whisper to Simone.

She turns to me, beaming. "Asha Jamil! I know it sucks that we can't go to the march, but we still get to meet her. Emily, we have to ask about her shoes!"

"Simone, the march is important," I say. "That's why I made the bonus episode."

"Well, I know other people should go. But they're not likely to host Asha, like we are," Simone says.

"I really think we should —"

She's not listening. As we weave through the hall toward math, she gasps, gripping my arm even harder. "Maybe we can get her on the podcast! Maybe we can ask her about her shoes WHILE SHE'S ON OUR PODCAST!"

Which is enough to remind me . . .

"I won't be allowed to do the podcast anymore."

Amelie catches up to us and butts in. "Speaking of the podcast . . . remember how Ms. Lydia and I met yesterday to talk about vegan lunch menus?"

I nod, even though this has nothing to do with Asha Jamil OR my potential demise.

"Well, Mr. Lau wouldn't even listen to us. He said he was in enough hot water with this CA Energy deal and the climate march, and he didn't have time to add vegan wing nuts to the mix."

Simone stops in mid hallway. "Vegan wing nuts! That is *très offensant*."

Amelie puffs her cheeks and blows a long, slow breath. "I was a little mad. Okay, I was furious. And, Emily, I was SO happy when you posted that bonus episode."

I stare from one to the other. Did they not hear the part where Mr. Lau was already freaking out about the climate march? The part that signaled my imminent expulsion?

"It was the right decision. Better to apologize later rather than ask permission first," Amelie says firmly.

Last week, I was so excited to hear Asha's name. And now, thoughts of Asha may as well be ash.

As we head toward the math room, I glance around the hall for Mr. Lau.

"Why haven't they called me to the office?" I ask Simone, as if she might be psychically connected.

Is it because they have to call my mom before they can officially expel me?

Simone shrugs. "They probably haven't heard your piece yet. The podcast isn't exactly the center of their universe, right? I bet they won't care as much as you think."

I only absorb the first sentence. They probably haven't heard it yet. That means Mr. Lau could listen at any moment. At any time during the day. I had no idea it was possible for all the blood in my body to stop moving, but that's what happens. It freezes in place.

Why did I want to post about the climate march in the first place? I'm an influencer! I'm supposed to be posting about fashion and home decor!

Mr. Gill puts us in pairs to discuss something. My eyes move over the page, but my brain absorbs nothing.

I think I have an ulcer.

There's no announcement. No messenger at the door. I make it to English without incident.

"Do you think so, Emily?" Reza asks, partway through the class.

"What?"

"The metaphor," Simone says. "We're talking about the metaphor, Em."

There's something in the poem about clouds and horses. A storm, maybe?

"Ooh, we should also write something about the words starting more softly," Simone says.

"And finishing like thunder," Reza adds.

On the list of things I never thought would happen: a discussion between Reza and Simone about metaphors and alliteration.

Was that the crackle of the PA system? Principal Lau must have heard the podcast by now. He'll know. Something will happen soon.

"Five more minutes," the teacher calls, as if predicting my doom.

"We're officially more fabulous than Emily at poetry," Simone says. She and Reza high-five across the desks.

I could run circles around any hoofbeat metaphors right now. There are horses thundering through my whole body.

How middle-school crises helped me learn to deal with life under pressure.

But nothing happens. It's almost lunchtime. I begin to think, cautiously, that everything will be okay. Maybe Mr. Lau decided a single podcast piece wasn't worth arguing about. Maybe I'm not in trouble.

Then, two minutes before the lunch bell, the summons comes. It's not a PA announcement or a messenger at the door. It's Mr. Chadwick himself. He doesn't say a thing. He crooks a finger at me, then points to Simone, too. We gather our books, apologize to the teacher, and leave. Somehow, my stomach stays behind, sitting at my desk.

Mr. Chadwick says nothing as we walk the infinite expanse of hallway.

"I'm glad your toothache's better," I venture.

He grunts. I can't tell whether it's a grunt with positive or negative connotations.

Simone's heels clack on the vinyl. One of my sneakers squeaks softly with every step. Mr. Chadwick's dress shoes are practically soundless. I wonder if teachers choose their shoes with these hallways in mind.

Approaching the principal's office feels like a movie sequence. Reception desk. Smiling Jennifers. Closed door. Mr. Chadwick knocks once, grasps the handle, and swings it open. There should be foreboding organ music.

"Good morning, girls," Principal Lau says, in a voice that contradicts his words. "Have a seat."

Mr. Chadwick moves behind the desk, where he leans against the wall with his arms crossed.

"We have procedures for a reason," Principal Lau is saying, folding his hands on the polished wood of his desk. "Our first priority is the safety of our students."

I shift in my plastic chair. "Mr. Lau, the climate crisis affects the long-term safety of students, which means —"

He holds up a palm. "Let me finish."

I try to read Mr. Chadwick's face, but it's perfectly blank. Maybe teachers choose their expressions the way they choose their shoes.

"This includes your safety," Mr. Lau says. "What if students left school to attend this march and they were lost, or injured? Technically, you could be held responsible."

Is that true?

"Stunts like this could jeopardize the new auditorium, which is something the school and the community both want," he says. "Is that your intention?"

My legs are quivering. I thought leg-quivering was something that happened in novels, but it's real. When I glance at Simone, her normally brown skin has turned pasty beige.

"I posted the episode," I blurt. "I take full responsibility for its content."

"Is that so?" Principal Lau peers at Simone.

When she glances at me, I can tell exactly what's happening inside her head. She doesn't want to abandon me.

"Mr. Lau, Simone wasn't even here," I insist. "She left after school for an appointment. You can check with Amelie."

Principal Lau nods slowly.

I open my mouth but I can't figure out what to say before he starts talking again.

"Well, Emily, I'm afraid there will be consequences. You'll be leaving this little podcast club of yours, effective immediately."

I knew it. But as I absorb his words, I realize something else. Even if the dates are changed, Mr. Lau is never going to choose me to meet Asha Jamil. It won't be me giving her a tour of the school. It won't be me snapping a selfie with her on the front steps, and going viral, and then influencing my thousands of followers. I've basically skewered my entire future by posting one podcast story.

A small sound escapes me. How embarrassing.

I try to sit straight-backed in my plastic chair and gaze directly at Mr. Lau, the way Emily Post would recommend. But it's particularly difficult to do this while telling myself, over and over again, not to cry.

Mr. Lau looks down his nose at me. "Your bonus episode has been deleted, and I'll trust you to keep other thoughts about the march to yourself. It's best not to interfere with things you're too young to understand."

He shifts his gaze. "Simone, you may consider this a warning. You won't get another."

"But Mr. Lau, *Cedarview Speaks* is —"

Principal Lau overrides her. "The podcast is meant to represent the voices of all our students, not the extreme opinions of a few."

Don't cry. Don't cry. Don't cry.

"Have I made myself clear?" The principal stares across his desk.

We nod mutely.

"I don't think we need to involve your parents at this stage. Do you?"

We shake our heads.

"Then you may go have your lunches."

Mr. Chadwick remains in the principal's office. He closes the door behind us.

I almost bang into the reception desk as we leave. My eyes have gone blurry.

"Are you okay, dear?" one of the Ms. Jennifers asks.

"Fine." My voice breaks, but Simone and I hurry away before she can ask any more questions.

I don't cry until we're inside the girls' washroom. I count that as a triumph. Although once we're among the safety of the stalls and sinks, I'm a blubbering mess.

"Okay, you have to stop," Simone says, handing me a piece of paper towel. "Do NOT let him make you cry. I'm so proud of what you did."

I hiccup. "I'm not upset."

Simone looks doubtful.

There are a hundred things I wish I'd said. I could have stood up, my chair clattering behind me. *I'm afraid I will have to resign because of editorial interference.* That's what I should have said.

"I'm not sad. I'm frustrated!" I blubber to Simone. "And I'm not sorry at all that I posted the podcast piece. I'm mad that Mr. Chadwick's on Mr. Lau's side. And . . ."

"That was censorship. You have every right to be rage-furious." She squeezes my arm. "Don't worry. We're going to figure out how to fix this. And in the meantime, the team will keep making the best podcast ever. Understood?"

I nod again, mostly so she'll let go of my shoulders. Outside, the hallway echoes with the shouts of kids heading toward the cafeteria.

"I wonder if Amelie will help, just until you're back?" Simone muses.

I was just beginning to calm down. I was starting to think she was right, and after a few weeks I'd be back on the podcast, and in the meantime I could talk to Mr. Chadwick and . . .

AMELIE? She's going to let Amelie take my place?

"Are you okay now? Should we go?" Simone asks.

I'm grinding my teeth so hard, it's difficult to speak.

"My eyes are too red," I manage to say. "You go ahead. I'll catch up in a few minutes."

She gives me one more squeeze, then she's gone.

I count to a hundred before I leave. A hundred long seconds of betrayal.

17

Trouble at the Top

All I want to do is curl up in my bed. I would pay a billion dollars just to pull the covers over my head. But when I get home, Ocean's waiting at the front door, bouncing up and down on his toes.

"I talked to Jackson," he says. "We're going to have our lemonade stand today."

I glance at the gray sky.

"Ocean, it's going to rain again. No one buys lemonade in the rain."

"Dad says we can do it if we have supervision."

"Great."

"But he's too busy."

"Oh, sorry."

Bed. Covers. Maybe Richard will make me hot chocolate. Why is Ocean still blocking my path?

"Two words," he says. "Bid. A."

"'Bidet' is one word."

"Then it's one big, dangerous word," he says.

Ugh. I had entirely forgotten the blackmail issue. I peer at Ocean. He has chalk smeared on his cheek and mud on his shirt. It's hard to take him seriously. Plus, I need to go inside. I need to think. Or refuse to think. Or something.

"Lemonade stands are for summer. Times when pedestrians are hot and need hydration," I tell him.

"One leeeetle call to Jackson ... or maybe Simone ..."

"You don't even have Simone's number."

"I could head over to Jackson's house right now. News of your butt wash could be all over the city." He makes flushing sounds. "*How do I turn it off?*" he mimics.

I grit my teeth. "Fine."

Ocean throws his arms around me, which is not an appropriate way to thank someone you've just blackmailed.

"LEMONADE STAND!" he hollers.

He races into the kitchen to tell Richard. "Emily's going to help us!"

I drop my backpack beneath the mocking eyes of the entranceway masks. Richard pops out of the kitchen to smile at me. "This is nice of you, Emily. I really appreciate it."

And, thus, I'm stuck with the eight-year-olds.

Ocean and Jackson have been begging to have this lemonade stand since we moved in, but Mom said they weren't allowed to unless someone was outside to supervise. First we were busy unpacking, and now no one wants to be outside with them because: NOT SUMMER.

Grumbling, I help Ocean maneuver a card table to the sidewalk. Then, while he collects Jackson, I prop a folding chair at the side of our townhouse, close enough to keep an eye on them, but far enough away that no one can possibly mistake me for a lemonade salesperson.

A moment later, Jackson wheels down the ramp from his front door, with Ocean jumping up and down behind his chair. Ever since we moved in, these two have been plotting world domination. This lemonade stand is probably their first step.

Jackson calls me over. "It's a little chilly out here," he says.

"Because it's not summer."

"I could really use a hot drink. And maybe a blanket."

Gritting my teeth even harder, I stomp inside. I grab a blanket from the couch and I invade Richard's space for long enough to make two cups of tea. But I microwave the water instead of boiling the kettle, because there are limits to what I'll do for two obnoxious eight-year-olds.

When I come back outside and set the mugs on the table, Jackson smiles. "Thanks, bidet. I mean, thanks, baby."

Both of which are EQUALLY INAPPROPRIATE!

I can't believe Ocean told him.

I glare at my pseudo-brother. "The only reason I'm supervising this stupid stand is because you blackmailed me," I hiss at him. "And since you already told, there's no reason for me to —"

"He could tell Simone," Jackson offers.

"You shouldn't say 'stupid,'" Ocean says at the same time.

"I committed murder after pushed to the brink by an eight-year-old's evil manipulations": the Emily Laurence story.

It would be impolite to strangle one's neighbor. It would also be impolite to strangle one's pseudo-brother. I repeat this to myself as I stomp away and throw myself into my chair. If I get hypothermia and gangrene and then my toes fall off, Ocean and Jackson will spend the rest of their lives feeling guilty about blackmailing me. Plus, they'll go bankrupt trying to sell iced beverages to freezing people.

Or not.

Just as I'm calculating how much longer I'll have to sit outside, a hockey dude saunters up the street with a huge sports bag slung over his shoulder. He's chewing a wad of gum so big I can see it from my lookout post. He's the exact opposite of a lemonade consumer.

He stops.

I can't hear what he's saying, but I watch him talk to the boys for a few minutes. Then he pulls out his wallet and searches through it. He asks a question. Ocean shakes his head. Then hockey dude shrugs and hands over five dollars.

FIVE DOLLARS.

I know it's five dollars, because while Jackson spins his chair in a sidewalk celebration, Ocean races over to wave the money under my nose.

My phone buzzes with a text from Daniella.

> My class was so great! The instructor was able to show me the places I went wrong with my code.

I quickly type back.

> Yay!

I have no idea what she's coding, but it can't hurt to be supportive.

Before I can text anything else, I'm distracted by action at the lemonade stand. A man with a baby stroller stops to buy a glass. Then Jackson's mom comes outside and buys herself a glass. Another neighbor arrives after that. A few minutes later, a woman with long, black braids buys two cups and drinks them both while chatting. Ocean and Jackson are apparently so fascinating, she pulls out a notebook to write down everything they say.

When Richard pops outside to check on things, she chats with him, too. Then she takes a picture of the boys! This is getting ridiculous.

Once she's gone and Richard's back inside, the boys wave me over.

"Every single person paid more than we asked!" Ocean says.

"I bet we made more money selling lemonade than you've ever made doing anything," Jackson says.

I resist the urge to smack him, which shows clear leadership potential on my part.

"Hey, a customer!" Ocean practically pushes me behind him before waving down the woman walking her dog across the street.

"Get your lemonade here!" he calls.

"All proceeds to a good cause!" Jackson adds.

The woman veers toward them.

"You're raising money for charity?" I ask.

"We're helping kids with disabilities," the boys say in unison, not to me but to the dog-walker. Sure enough, she pulls out her wallet and hands over another five bucks.

Now I'm less astounded that people are buying lemonade, but still shocked.

"That's actually impressive," I tell the boys, once their customer has left.

"If you help, we can do it again tomorrow!" Ocean says.

"Not *that* impressive." But still, it's possible my pseudo-brother and his friend aren't entirely evil.

"Maybe sometime soon," I say. That's all it takes to have both of them beaming.

An hour later, once they've counted and recounted their earnings, Jackson and Ocean pack up. And by "pack up," I mean they take their sign and the rest of their lemonade into Jackson's house. Jackson looks back and says, "You probably want to put away the table, right?" Then he makes water-squirting and toilet-flushing noises, and both he and Ocean giggle like maniacs.

It would be impolite to strangle one's neighbor.

Ocean talks all through dinner, and everything he says is "Lemonade stand...Jackson...lemonade stand...Jackson..."

"Can we talk about something else?" I ask finally.

"What?" Ocean says.

For a moment, I imagine what would happen if I blurted out everything about my day. The disgrace of being fired from the podcast. The realization that I'll never get to meet Asha Jamil. The fork-in-the-heart feeling of Amelie replacing me on *Cedarview Speaks*.

My throat starts to close as I think of it. If I tell them, I'll burst into tears. And it won't do any good anyway. Mom will say I should have used more official channels to protest the decision about my climate march story. She'll tell me to write a letter, or some other ultra-polite thing.

"Emily?"

Everyone's staring at me.

"You wanted to change the subject?" Mom prompts.

Of course, I can't think of any normal conversation topics on such short notice.

"School," she suggests. "How was class this week, Ocean?"

"Jackson says school is basically prison for kids," Ocean says.

"Jackson is the most annoying ever." I'm definitely not over the fact he called me Bidet/Babe.

"That's not nice to say. That's prejudiced against people in wheelchairs," Ocean says.

"Ocean, it is not. And you're the second most annoying!"

I admit, this is not polite. But Ocean would make anyone lose control of her manners.

"Emily," Mom says, with her warning voice.

"Prejudiced, prejudiced, prejudiced," Ocean chants.

"Settle down," Richard says. "Who wants more soup?"

"Prejudiced," Ocean whispers.

"I'm prejudiced against Jackson because he's a jerk, not because he's in a wheelchair!"

Richard turns from the stove. "Jackson has a lot of challenges."

Mom nods. "It wouldn't kill you to be patient, Emily."

Which is ridiculous because I *am* patient, and also because it *might* kill me.

"You have no idea what —"

And then Ocean makes flushing sounds.

It really might kill me.

"My mom always said world peace begins at home," Richard says.

This makes him the third most annoying person, though I don't say that out loud.

Then he passes me another bowl of chicken tortilla soup, which he's simmered all day. It's one of the most melt-in-your-mouth things he's ever created.

But not vegan.

"Prejudiced," Ocean chants again.

"Enough. Let's move on," Richard says. "Eat your dinner."

I'm still staring at my bowl, inhaling cayenne and cilantro.

"Everything okay?" Richard asks.

"Fine."

I'm the worst vegan in the history of the world. And I posted a link to a vegan website this week, which makes me a huge hypocrite. But everyone knows that an influencer's online persona is not exactly the same as her real-life identity. Right?

Richard's soup is delicious.

But what if I *am* a hypocrite? What if I'm a hypocrite the same way as Mr. Chadwick, who basically sold our podcast to CA Energy? Or Mr. Lau, who seems to have sold the whole school?

I watch Mom and Ocean devouring their servings, but I can't eat any more.

"May I be excused?" I ask.

"Are you feeling okay?" Mom's eyebrows wrinkle in the middle.

She used to look at me that way more often. I used to be the only thing she worried about in the whole world.

"Just tired."

A few minutes later, I finally get to climb into bed and pull the covers over my head.

18

Tragedy of Tragedies

Curled beneath my duvet, I stare at Asha Jamil's YouHappy stream. She has another new set of silk sheets in a bright turquoise blue. She photographed them with blue flowers in a white vase on her white end table. It's gorgeous. But it all seems a little empty compared to the fact that she's being used as a climate march alternative.

Does she know?

I'm itching to ask her.

@realAshaJamil, do you know Cedarview Middle School is USING your appearance to keep kids from speaking up against climate change?

But I don't type that, because even though my mom thinks I'm incapable of using social media, I do understand that I can't put the name of my school into a public post. And Asha doesn't follow me — yet — so I can't send her a direct message.

Although . . . maybe there's a contact form on her website? There is!

I sit up, throwing off the covers. Before I can get nervous, I tap out a message.

Dear Asha,
I'm a huge fan, and so excited that you're planning to visit Cedarview Middle School. Hopefully, I'll be chosen to give you a tour of the school and I can tell you — in person! — how you've inspired me to become a social media influencer.
But, as one influencer to another, I need to warn you about something. The principal of Cedarview is using your visit to keep kids away from a climate march, scheduled for the same day. Which isn't fair at all! I know you're dedicated to saving the Earth, just like I am. Can you change your visit back to Thursday, so kids can be inspired by you AND be inspired to march?
Sincerely, your biggest admirer,
Emily Laurence

Mom slips into my room.

I quickly turn off my screen and toss my phone onto my pillow. "I'm about to start my homework."

She sits on the edge of my bed beside me.

"I know it's not easy to be a big sister," she says. "I was a big sister once, remember? And your Auntie Kay used to get so much attention, you wouldn't believe it."

My Auntie Kay lives in Toronto. She wears pantsuits and black leather pumps and owns a Simone-sized collection of handbags.

"Auntie Kay was never as annoying as Ocean."

"Oh, you'd be surprised," Mom says.

Is it possible my mom is blinded by love, and she can't see how irritating Ocean can be?

"This is a big transition, and it's going to take some time," she says. "But Richard and I think you two should spend more time together. So from now on, Friday afternoons are going to be your time."

Um... what?

"You're a mature, responsible teen now. You can easily watch Ocean one afternoon a week."

Friday afternoon? But this is already Wednesday!

How my life was ruined by my rabid pseudo-sibling.

Mom's still talking. "Richard and I have been needing some alone time. We'll schedule early dinners on Fridays, and you and Ocean can bond. Maybe watch a movie together, or play a board game, or —"

"Mom, I have things to do!"

"Nothing's more important than family, sweetheart. And this is non-negotiable."

She hugs my unresponsive, fallen-into-a-shock-induced-coma body.

Then she turns, as if by accident, and picks up my phone from my pillow.

What is she doing?

She keys in my access code.

"Simone says Mr. Chadwick has a crush on Ms. Flores," I blurt. Anything to distract her.

She chuckles. "Really? How about you and Simone? Any crushes?"

"Mom!"

"Hmmm..." she says.

I don't think she's referring to the teacher drama. Because she's opened YouHappy now.

"Emily . . . have you been . . . *posting photos*?" She says it as if she can barely believe it. She says it as if "photos" is a swear word.

"Hardly at all!" I say. "It was an accident."

"You're posting photos of yourself on social media by accident."

When Mom's voice gets quiet and flat, things are bad.

"I typed in a post, imagining what it would be like. Then Marcus at school interrupted me and I accidentally pressed the post button. After that, since I'd already posted, I added a few more important things."

"Things like '*Asha's shoes are seriously the best. I can't wait to show her mine.*'" Mom's voice is still quiet and flat.

But she doesn't understand. "As an influencer, you can't post only about important things. You have to win your audience with fun and engaging content, and then you add more serious issues. If you watch The Palette Pixie's video I have up . . ."

She's not listening. My phone is locked in her hand, and her arms are crossed.

"Emily, I am so disappointed in you."

I stop talking.

"I can't even believe you would do this." She shakes her head.

"I'm sorry, but —"

She puts a hand up. "Not one more word. I'm going to have to think more about this. In the meantime, your phone has become my phone. And there will be NO social media."

This is so unfair!

"Wait! Can I just text Simone and —"

She gives me a look. A look that says I might never text Simone ever again for the rest of my life.

Then she leaves, closing the door behind her.

Of course, the first thing I want to do is call Simone and tell her everything. But our only landline is downstairs and I have NO PHONE! And Simone's probably texting with Amelie right now, anyway, planning their next podcast episode.

I fling myself back onto my bed.

My life is basically ruined.

And that's when I remember the very worst part.

EVERY FRIDAY WITH OCEAN!

Last time she left us alone, I almost flooded the house and froze my private parts. Now she wants me to spend an evening with him every single week? I don't think I can survive.

The more I think about her words, the angrier I get. She knows I'm responsible enough for social media and she knows it's my future dream job. She should be supporting me! She pretended the Friday evening plan was all about Ocean and me bonding, but it's really about her going out with Richard. And did Mom really say "Nothing's more important than family"? Because I WAS HER FAMILY! And then she dragged me out of my apartment — an apartment where no eight-year-old ever, ever stunk up the bathroom or missed the toilet bowl and left dribbles of yellow across the tile floor. She dragged me out of that apartment and my happy life and into this ridiculous townhouse, equipped with bidets and overrun by hooligans.

How my existence basically ended before it began.

But there's no sense even thinking in social media posts. At this rate, I won't be allowed to share anything until I'm eighty. Simone and Amelie will be fabulous podcast cohosts, and they'll bond online, and Asha Jamil will have everyone starstruck, and no one will even remember the climate march, and the world will end.

My eyes fall on my copy of *Etiquette*. But I already know there's no entry on how to handle censorship at school and someone controlling all your freedom of expression at home. Life is a lot more complicated now than it was a hundred years ago.

I can't believe my mother took away my phone and caused the end of civilization.

19

The Bathroom of Abandonment

Simone finds me as soon as I arrive at school in the morning. She's wearing a black beret, as if she's planning to paint watercolors in a French park.

"You didn't reply to my texts!"

"My mom confiscated my phone," I tell her.

She gasps. "*Très terrible!*"

"And that's not the worst part. Now that Mr. Lau kicked me off the podcast, he's never going to let me meet —"

But Simone's not listening. She's focused on her screen. "Amelie and I recorded the vegan club interview last night and we shared the file with you. Did you listen?"

"No phone." Maybe she didn't grasp the severity of this situation?

"But you can listen on mine!" she says. "We have just enough time before class."

Then Daniella and Amelie show up, and there's no choice but to press play on Simone's screen.

Amelie: Welcome to *Cedarview Speaks*, our school podcast! All the news you need. We're your hosts today, Amelie Cattaneo and . . .

Simone: Simone Ahn. Thanks for tuning in. You might have met Amelie in the hallways this fall. She's new to the school, but she's already shaking things up.

Amelie: I'm so happy to be here!

Simone: Amelie is launching a vegan club at Cedarview, and today she'll tell us all about it.

Amelie: Thank you for having me, Simone! I've only been at Cedarview for a few weeks, and I'm already a big fan of the podcast. I'm so happy to be here to talk about the importance of the vegan lifestyle. I mean, do you want to eat what is basically an animal carcass, or do you want to eat something that's good for you and good for the Earth?

Simone: How long have you been a vegan, Amelie?

Amelie: Since birth. Well, since before birth, really, because my parents are both vegan, too.

Simone: So what changes do you hope to see around Cedarview? What will the vegan club be working toward?

Amelie: Ms. Lydia and I have already met with the principal. CoastFresh doesn't have a vegan line yet, but it's something they might consider for our cafeteria in the future.

Simone: That sounds so exciting, Amelie. For those of us who care a lot about climate change, things like vegan menus are an obvious choice. Good job helping us change the world!

Amelie: Thanks!

Simone: Well, that's all the time we have for *Cedarview Speaks* this week. Thanks for joining Amelie and me. And please tune in next week for all the news you need!

I pass Simone's phone back to her.
"It's perfect," I say.
"It wasn't EXACTLY perfect the first time," Simone says. "Because when Amelie said 'carcass,' I was taking a sip from my water bottle, and I sprayed water all over the mixer. And then I had to take off my sweatshirt to wipe it up before it damaged anything, but luckily I was wearing another shirt underneath, and . . ."
She keeps talking. And talking.
Amelie bumps her shoulder gently.
"Tell Emily what Mr. Lau said," she prompts.
I look up. Did they talk to Mr. Lau about me? Is it possible that . . .

But Simone looks uncomfortable.

"I know you were really excited about meeting Asha Jamil," she says. "But Mr. Lau said Amelie and I can interview Asha on Friday."

I deserve a gold medal or a Nobel Prize or approximately a billion dollars for forcing a smile onto my face.

"That's great."

"Oh, I'm so glad you're not mad," Simone says. "Because ... ASHA JAMIL!"

She and Amelie squeal and bounce up and down together. Daniella claps her hands over her ears.

"The schedule's too tight for October, so Asha will have to be in November's episode, but —"

"Simone!" It comes out as a bark, and she instantly stops squealing. I take a breath and try for my normal voice. "Could I borrow you for a minute? I need to talk about something."

I know I'm being kind of rude to Daniella and Amelie, but I can't help it. I need Simone to focus, and she's never going to do that with vegan manga eyes distracting her.

Thankfully, she follows me to the bathroom.

"I never told you *why* I posted my story about the climate march."

I tell her everything I heard Mr. Lau say in the office. I tell her how he implied that by distracting starry-eyed girls, he could control the whole student body and keep everyone away from the climate march. And with every word I repeat, I'm more offended.

Simone's silent.

"I know," I tell her. "It's completely shocking, right?"

She nods slowly. "But . . ."

Um . . . what? There is no "but." There is absolutely no "but" about this situation, unless she's going to call Mr. Lau a butt-face, which would be accurate but extremely impolite.

It's my turn to fall silent.

"My mom said she couldn't drive me to the climate march anyway. She's busy on Friday."

"Simone, you can't drive to a climate march. Unless maybe you have an electric car. We have to bike or take the bus together."

"And Mr. Lau said that Amelie and I could interview Asha. Like, actually meet her and ask her questions."

"You're going to throw away the future of the world because you get to meet Asha Jamil?"

Simone folds her arms. "Emily, this is a huge opportunity! You would do the same thing if you hadn't been kicked off the podcast. It's not like you've ever cared about climate change before."

I open my mouth and close it. Open it and close it. I'm as articulate as the library goldfish.

"I CARE!" I manage, finally.

"Since when?"

"Since always! Of course I care. The world is ending! We made posters. We started a whole juice-box recycling program last year, remember? Just because I don't wear vegan pleather doesn't mean I don't care about climate change!"

"Are you sure? Because it seems like you're mad that Amelie gets to interview Asha Jamil instead of you. You've been jealous ever since Amelie got here."

"That's ridiculous!" And completely unfair.

"You never liked her from the start," Simone repeats.

"SHE HAS PERFECT HAIR!"

I admit, this is not a good argument. But this is what comes out of my mouth.

"Amelie says that commenting about other people's hair and clothes is a way we reinforce the patriarchy."

I'm not even sure what that means, and it's too late to be reasonable now.

"And I say that when people use French words and wear stupid French hats, they're acting like giant suck-ups!"

The bathroom door swings open and Ms. Flores pokes her head in.

"Goodness, girls. Everything okay in here?"

I am not okay. Tears are streaming down my cheeks entirely without my permission. I whirl away, shut myself in a stall, and grab a wad of toilet paper.

"Sorry, Ms. Flores. We're fine," Simone says, her voice cold.

"Emily?" Ms. Flores calls.

"I'm fine," I mumble through the paper wad.

"Well, I'll be in the classroom if you want to chat," she says.

She leaves.

Simone heads for the door too, but she pauses. "I know you're disappointed about the march, and about not meeting Asha."

My insides soften. I open my mouth to apolo —

"But this is a huge opportunity for me, and a real friend would support me," Simone says.

And then she's gone. I have been officially abandoned to make my way alone down the rocky path toward climate justice.

20

Top Ten Terrible Days Ever

I wish I could explain this whole situation to my mom. Maybe she would be horrified about the way Mr. Lau is keeping kids from the climate march. But I can't tell her. She's already mad at me about my YouHappy posts. If she hears that I posted a podcast episode without permission, she might be twice as furious. I won't get my phone back for a decade.

Richard and Ocean are having a kitchen dance party, so I sit on the front stoop trying to think of some way to fix everything. I need to make Simone change her mind about the Asha interview, make Mr. Lau reconsider his career choices, go to the climate march and get pulled on stage to give an impromptu speech, thus influencing thousands of people even though I don't have a phone . . .

I could call Mya. She might have some ideas. Unfortunately, her contact info is on my cellphone.

Before my head can explode, the car door slams and Mom rushes up the walk.

"Emily! Wait 'til you hear!" She's beaming. She has a stack of newspapers tucked under one arm.

She steps around me to open the front door. "Richard? Ocean? Are you home?" she calls. "You have to see this."

They emerge from the kitchen looking sweaty. Ocean wears a chocolate milk mustache.

"Ocean, you're famous!" Mom says.

He looks supremely un-famous.

She pulls a newspaper from under her arm and unfurls it. There, on the front page of the *West Side Community News*, is a picture of Jackson and Ocean. They wear matching grins.

"Top 10 Under 10," the headline reads. "Meet the city's rising stars."

"Whaaaat?" Ocean presses close to Mom and tries to read over her elbow. "I'm a rising star!"

"I met that reporter when she stopped by. Let's hear what she has to say," Richard says, grinning.

"Read it! Read it! Read it!" Ocean chants.

So while I look to the entranceway masks for possible life-saving advice, Mom clears her throat.

Top 10 Under 10
BY ETERNITY WILLIAMS

These two might seem small for social entrepreneurs, but their lemonade stand — the first in a series of planned fundraising efforts — is dedicated to making life better for those with disabilities. Jackson Johnston was born with cerebral palsy. He has inspired best friend and playmate Ocean Patterson to lend a hand. When this reporter stopped by the stand on Wednesday afternoon, the youngsters had already raised more than $35 for their cause — this despite inclement weather. Both 8-year-olds have a bright future in our community.

Mom, Richard, and Ocean exchange a flurry of high-fives.

"Well? What do you think, Emily?" Mom asks.

"Impressive."

In actuality, I don't think that last sentence was at all appropriate, because journalists are supposed to be objective and they're supposed to report only the facts. There is no scientific way to know whether Ocean and Jackson have a bright future in our community. They could end up in a juvenile detention center.

"You boys did such a good job of that lemonade stand," Mom gushes.

I suppose this is true. And the hole where one of Ocean's teeth used to be is fairly adorable in print.

Mom brought home six copies of the newspaper. Once she's finished gushing, I take one and read the rest of the article. Also on the "Top 10 Under 10" list: an animal shelter volunteer, a violin prodigy, two gymnasts, a kid who mows lawns for his elderly neighbors, a competitive swimmer, a chess player, and a pianist. For the first time ever, I wish I were "Under 10."

"This calls for something special. We're going to celebrate," Richard says. "I'll make dessert."

But Ocean has stopped listening. He makes a grab for Mom's phone, which she's left on the entranceway table. A minute later, he's pointing the thing at me.

"What are you . . ."

Too late.

"Ha! Got you. Your hair's hilarious."

I look to Mom for help, but she's laughing.

"You do look like a ragamuffin," she says.

That is not a real word . . . is it? Anyway, it's not my fault that I tend to pull at my hair when I'm stressed.

"Rag-a-muffin, rag-a-muffin," Ocean repeats, over and over, as I stomp up the stairs toward my room.

I do not slam my bedroom door.

I shut it.

Firmly.

Friday. Phoneless Friday. As soon as I wake up, I remember it's exactly one week until the climate march, and Asha Jamil's visit, and the world basically ending.

When I get to school, Simone pretends nothing's happened between us. So I do the same.

I drop my eraser in math class, and she passes it to me.

When Bryce looks like he's about to sit beside Daniella in social studies, the two of us flank her, and Amelie scurries to grab the seat behind.

When Simone and Amelie talk about wearing matching shirts to their Asha interview, I tell them it's a great idea.

And when Amelie passes around a container of vegan carrot muffins at lunchtime, I take one. They're surprisingly good, but not quite tasty enough to make me forget that I'm being left out of all media influence, especially when Reza stops by the table to talk about the podcast.

"Oh, Emily can't help at lunch," Amelie tells him. "But I can give you a hand. Anytime."

For some reason, Reza looks unhappy with this offer.

"Why is Amelie the producer now?" he asks me. "I thought you —"

"She's doing a great job," I say, forcing my lips to make some sort of smile shape.

I try to think about other things. I think about how much better the CoastFresh logos would look if they weren't so royally blue. I think about how long it must take Ms. Lydia to scrape her hair into that bun every morning. I think of everything I can that's not podcast-related.

But Simone is distractingly loud.

Apparently, Mr. Lau wants to be more involved in the podcast now, and he stopped her between classes to comment on her story list.

"He says he's had enough of all the 'climate change fear-mongering,'" she says, using air quotes. "He doesn't even want us to run our story about the vegan club."

Reza groans. "Is that what got you in trouble, Emily? The climate march thing? I thought that was sorta great. And a couple people have told me they're going to the march now."

Which is nice to hear, even if it's just from Reza. A couple of people have told me the same thing. My smile is slightly more authentic this time.

"It's firmly established that climate change is caused by human activity," Amelie says, "and 97 percent of scientists agree."

"Obviously," Reza says.

Daniella wilts beside me. Poor thing. Climate change can cause a lot of anxiety.

I butt in. "What did Mr. Lau say, exactly?"

"Absolutely no controversy this week," Simone says. "Keep it simple."

"And he thinks vegan food is controversial?"

"I guess?" Simone shrugs.

Daniella looks as if she's hoping to disappear under the table. "CoastFresh is owned by CA Energy," she whispers.

"CA Energy owns CoastFresh?" I repeat.

Everyone turns to stare at her.

"What? How do you know?" Amelie asks.

"CA Energy is heavily invested in fertilizers for feed crops," Daniella says.

We all lean closer to hear.

"Those are crops that are used to feed livestock, like cattle. And cattle becomes beef. Beef becomes cheeseburgers. So you can see how a move toward a plant-based diet could be seen as controversial."

Daniella has never said so many words in a row, ever. And most of those words were audible. Maybe we've been a good influence on her.

Reza smacks the table. "This sucks."

Simone looks momentarily hopeful. "Basketball isn't controversial. There must be some sort of basketball story?"

He ponders for a minute. "New point guard."

I don't think Simone has any idea what a point guard is, but she nods enthusiastically. "Sounds perfect."

"I'm not sure that's what Daniella was suggesting," I say.

"True. What about the climate thing?" Reza says.

Is it possible he's capable of rational thought?

Simone ignores us both.

"So we have a sports story." She ticks it off on her fingers. "We have the poem by the seventh-graders. And the secretary asked if we can remind people to return their field trip permission slips more promptly."

"Great," Amelie says. "We'll do a story on that."

I think she's being sarcastic, but Simone nods.

"We'll record the replacement story on Monday. If Daniella can do all the post-production in one day, we can get the episode out on Wednesday, exactly on time."

I can't listen anymore. Besides, I was about to open my thermos when I remembered that Richard packed pork curry inside it this morning. And since I can't contribute to this podcast conversation anyway . . .

"I'm going to the bathroom," I tell them.

No one seems to notice when I leave.

I head for the foyer bathrooms and lock myself safely into a stall. It's really not necessary to eat in the cafeteria every day. There's something to be said for enjoying one's food alone, in peace. I may have found the perfect solution to my vegan issues.

How I learned to embrace solitude and reap the rewards.
Not that I'll ever be allowed to post that.

As I'm taking my second solitary, phone-free bite, the door to the bathroom swings open.

"And then she said she doesn't believe in homework and . . . ew . . . what's that smell?" It's Amelie's voice.

"Curry." That's Simone.

What are they doing here?

I panic. I screw the lid back onto my thermos and search for a place to stash it. The only option is the metal container for disposing feminine hygiene products. Even though that's obviously unsanitary, I try stuffing my lunch inside it. It won't fit. I get the bottom edge of the thermos wedged in. Then it's stuck.

"Who's in here?" Simone calls.

"Just me." I try to sound light and breezy, as if I get caught hiding in bathroom stalls every afternoon.

"Why does it smell like food?"

"I know! It was like that when I came in." I frantically pull toilet paper off the roll and arrange it on top of my thermos. Then I flush the toilet.

Not fast enough. Simone's face appears above the stall. Amelie's appears on the other side. Which is gross. I mean, it's one thing for Simone and me to talk like this, because we've been doing it for years, but what kind of person blatantly invades another person's bathroom space?

"This is hilarious. Do you two talk like this all the time?" Amelie grins down at me.

"Nope, and I'm all done here." I stand up before either of them can wonder why I'm sitting fully dressed on the toilet seat. Then I push out of the stall and make a big production out of washing my hands, while Amelie shuts herself in the neighboring stall. (Not the one with the thermos, thank goodness). Her monologue about using zucchini strings as noodles almost covers the sound of her peeing.

I catch Simone's eye in the mirror while I'm flicking the water from my hands. She's staring at me.

"You're not even trying to be vegan. You've been eating meat this whole time," she whispers.

"You get this thing called a spiralizer and you feed in the whole zucchini," Amelie calls, from inside her stall.

"You ate a cheeseburger!" I hiss.

"ONCE! Because I was HUNGRY!"

"What? Are you still hungry?" Amelie asks, joining us at the sinks. Her manga eyes flick from me to Simone and back again.

I was kidding myself about the bathroom being a lunchtime option. There's nothing uplifting about eating in a bathroom. Also, I was only a few bites into Richard's pork and now I'm going to starve for the rest of the day. There's no way to retrieve my thermos with Amelie washing her hands and Simone staring at me as if I'm the world's biggest fraud.

But it's difficult to make good decisions when one's phone has been confiscated, the world is ending, and no one else seems to care.

"I'd better get ready for class," Simone says.

"I'll come," Amelie says.

She flips her hair. Seriously!

Neither of them glances back at me as they swoop out the door.

I've always assumed that Simone will write my biography, once she's a famous fashion designer and has excellent art-world connections. She'll dress in a sleek black suit, notebook open on the table between us. She'll use a voice recorder as well, because sometimes my stories will be so fascinating, she'll forget to move her pen.

This will all happen in my New York penthouse, obviously.

Except that it won't. Now I'll have to create an *autobiography*. That's the only way I'll get to choose what's included. I can't trust it to a vegan fashion designer. She won't have an audience anyway because who wants to wear fake leather? It's just expensive plastic.

My whole life plan has crumbled.

21

The Lyingest Liars of Lyingville

Marcus finds me wandering the hallway. The bell's going to ring soon. I should probably grab my books from my locker. But I'm worried Simone and Amelie will be standing there, talking about Asha, Asha, and Asha. It's exactly one week until her visit. And one week until the climate march, too.

"You look lost," Marcus says.

I sigh, giving my eyes a quick scrub with the back of my hand.

"I'm okay, Marcus. I'm not lost. Just a little . . . confused. And tired of school."

He nods knowingly. Then he leans closer.

"Do you want to see some escape pods?"

I almost laugh, but I catch myself just in time. I may as well see his hiding spots. It's possible that Marcus is my only remaining friend.

"Okay. Let's go," I tell him.

"Great." Then he stops and raises one hand. "BUT you

can't reveal them to anyone else. And if you find any other useful hiding spots, I would appreciate hearing about them."

"Deal."

So we embark on the most unusual school tour ever.

"You already know about the beanbag chairs," he says.

I nod. That's where I should have had my lunch. What was I thinking?

"The entire library is an excellent hiding spot, as long as you keep moving and remain one or two shelves away from a teacher at all times. Last month, Ms. Flores was in there a lot, but she hasn't been around lately."

Interesting.

We march onward, and Marcus points out the computer server room (occasionally left unlocked) and the third-floor teachers' bathroom.

"There's a broken stall in there. The door's nailed closed, but if you crawl underneath and keep your feet up on the toilet lid, you're basically invisible."

Next, he shows me how to push up and left against the door of the book storage closet in the main hall. The latch gives way.

"I had a good spot in the art room, too, but it's been compromised."

I guess that was the time he disappeared for most the day, and they found him behind the kiln.

When the bell rings, we're near the cafeteria again.

"I'd better get to social studies," I say.

He nods and turns the other way.

"Marcus, where are you going? What class do you have?"

He shrugs. "I'm heading for the cafeteria," he whispers. "Sometimes Ms. Lydia and I share cookies and talk about space."

Ms. Lydia shares cookies?

I head for class, thinking that the world is a more unusual place than I ever would have expected.

Ms. Truby loves long class discussions about ethics. Today, she's picked a particularly terrible topic.

Lying. And whether it's ever okay to lie.

"When might omission count as a lie?" she asks.

I shoot my hand into the air. "If you know something's important, but you choose to ignore it, does that count as a lie?"

I feel Simone's glare burning into me, but I don't even look in her direction.

Daniella puts her hand up.

"Daniella?" Ms. Truby sounds surprised. This is probably the only time Daniella has ever volunteered an answer in class. I'm starting to think she's had a serious personality change.

"May I go to the bathroom?"

Well, that was anticlimactic.

"Of course," Ms. Truby says. "Does anyone else have something to say about the topic?"

"Presenting yourself online can be like lying," Simone says. "You have to choose which part of yourself you want to share."

"But that's the whole point of social media. Building a persona," I say.

"For some people," Simone mutters. "People who pretend to be best friends and then don't even care when the other person's excited about something."

"I think we might be getting slightly off topic here," Ms. Truby says. "Do you think —"

"I think YouHappy should have its heart button, and its comment button, and a big LIAR button at the bottom," Simone says.

"Which you would have no reason to use," I say.

"I would use it on your vegan post, right this second."

"Girls, let's pause this for a moment and see what someone else has to say." Ms. Truby scans the classroom, looking a little desperate. "Amelie, what do you think?"

Amelie's manga eyes go even wider than usual, and she fades from porcelain white to pasty white.

"Do you think it's ever okay to lie?" Ms. Truby asks.

"No!" With that, Amelie grabs her notebook, pushes her chair back, and runs from the room.

"Oh dear," Ms. Truby says. She reaches back until she finds the edge of her desk, then she leans against it.

Reza pipes up. "Bryce lied to me once."

"Really?" Ms. Truby says.

"I asked how he did in the cross-country race. He said he came second. Then, when I said congratulations, he whispered —"

"Second to last!" Bryce cackles.

They both collapse into giggles.

Ms. Truby puts her fingers to her temple. "Maybe we'll continue this another time. Could someone check on Daniella and Amelie, please?"

I start to get up. "I'll go."

"No, *I'll* go," Simone says. "Otherwise, we may never find out the truth."

Simone doesn't talk to me for the rest of the day, but Daniella and Amelie both return to class. Daniella says that something at lunch gave her a stomach-ache, and Amelie says the same thing happened to her.

No one asks whether they're lying.

Things are fairly quiet after that, until we're in science together. I'm sitting beside Daniella, as usual, but she's paying no attention to Ms. Flores. Instead, she's staring over her shoulder at Bryce.

So I stare too.

And I see it. He's copying work off the kid sitting beside him.

Great. Now Simone and Amelie and I have two people to protect.

I'm about to lean across Daniella and nudge Simone when I remember we're not speaking. And I'm sort of scared to lean across Daniella right now, anyway. She's gritting her teeth together so hard I can hear the grinding.

"I saw him," I tell her, as soon as the bell rings. "He shouldn't be —"

But Daniella's not listening. She walks straight for Ms. Flores's desk. Then Simone and Amelie swoosh out of the classroom with their arms linked, giggling at something. Or someone. And I leave all by myself. Which is fine. Emily Post says that the attributes of a great lady are sincerity, simplicity, sympathy, and serenity. So I leave the school by myself. And I simply and sincerely refuse to think about the lack of sympathy being shown by some people I might mention, if I weren't so serene.

I'm barely out the door when a horn beep gets my attention. Mom's idling by the curb.

"I thought we'd go for a little drive," she says, when I climb into the car. "We can talk about this social media thing."

That sounds ominous. Also . . .

"Don't you have to get Ocean from martial arts?"

"What?"

"Ocean? Martial arts?" I repeat.

Usually his class is on Thursday, but this morning Richard said something about an extra session.

"Darn it! I forgot," Mom says. Though she doesn't actually say "darn."

I don't even know why they send Ocean to karate. It doesn't seem to dampen his energy level AT ALL. And what if Daniella's dad is right about karate making people more assertive? The last thing we need is an extra-assertive version of Ocean.

"Busy day." Mom sighs. "Well, you and I can chat on the way to the dojo."

Great. Just great.

"Text Richard for me, would you?" she says, digging in her purse for her phone and passing it to me without taking her eyes from the road.

I key in her password. "What should I tell him?"

"Tell him we're still on for our Friday date, but I'll be a bit late getting home," she says.

I click on Richard's name, at the top of Mom's stream of texts. And that's when the most psychologically scarring, seriously atrocious thing EVER happens. Obviously, I don't MEAN to read Mom's private communications. But when I click on Richard's name, his most recent texts appear, and . . .

"AHHHHHHHHHHHH!" Any remaining scraps of my serenity are lost forever.

Mom slams on the brakes. "What?"

Someone honks behind us.

"YOU'VE BEEN SEXTING!"

"What?" This seems to be Mom's only word.

More honking from behind us. Mom pulls over and grabs for her phone.

"For heaven's sake, Emily. Not everything has to be an emotional emergency."

She finally reads her screen, then turns a bright pink.

"I didn't mean to see them," I say. When you glance at a screen, you can't help absorbing a few key words, and when one of those words is BREASTS and when that word is repeated THREE TIMES, you're bound to notice. "I can never un-read that, you know."

Mom flushes, but she presses her lips together and pulls back into traffic.

I wait for a minute . . . a long minute . . . but then I can't hold it in any longer.

"I can't believe you took away my phone because you think I'm going to post naked pictures or something, and meanwhile you're SEXTING!"

"It's not as if you've never seen the word 'breast' before," she says.

"MOM!"

"I'd hardly call it sexting."

"That is SO COMPLETELY sexting. He's texting you about how much he likes your private parts. That's the definitive definition of sexting."

"Fine. I'll ask Richard to refrain from texting about my breasts."

"Stop saying that word!"

"If you'd stay off my phone —" Mom says.

"You told me to text Richard!"

A woman takes a step off the sidewalk onto the crosswalk and then jumps back, saving her own life.

"We'll talk about this later," Mom tells me.

Great. I can't wait for Mom to explain why I can't post perfectly innocent selfies on social media, but it's okay for her to get SEXTING SEXTS!

I'm serious about psychological trauma. The rest of the way to Ocean's dojo, all I can think about is the fact that Richard loves my mom's . . . ARGH!

And as soon as we park, she makes another attempt at a heart-to-heart.

"About the texts you saw . . ."

"Mom, I don't ever want to talk about this again," I say.

"I think it's important that you understand some things are not appropriate for kids. But for adults, expressing healthy sexuality —"

Did she seriously just say that word? I clap my hands over my ears and start singing "Mary Had a Little Lamb." Which is possibly not my most mature move ever but is absolutely necessary.

She stops.

After a few minutes, I decide it's fair to point out her hypocrisy. "If you'll scroll through my YouHappy posts, you'll find I used the site perfectly appropriately."

"Emily, don't even dream about getting your phone back for at least a week. We need to talk about these issues. Calmly."

I fold my arms. She folds her arms.

This is definitely not good parenting on her part.

Finally, after what seems like hours, Ocean emerges, sweaty and smiling. He dives into the back seat.

"We did power punches today. Power punches and blocks!"

"Great," Mom says.

"Bam! Bam! Bam! Kablam!" Ocean shouts.

For once, I don't even mind. I have nothing else to speak to my mother about. And he'll have to say "kablam" fifty more times to erase the word "breasts" from my eyelids.

22

Sugar Rush

When we get home, Richard is helping Jackson's dad put the finishing touches on a ramp to our back door.

"This is wonderful," Mom says. "Now Jackson can pop by anytime."

My life is a horror movie.

"He's already inside, waiting to play video games with Ocean," Richard says.

"And we brought over some pizza," Jackson's dad says. "The least we can do, when you've all been so kind to him. You especially, Emily."

I quickly plaster on a polite smile.

"She's a good egg," Mom says, putting an arm around my shoulders. So I guess our fight is over. And I guess I'm babysitting both Ocean *and* Jackson. Because that's the way my life is going these days.

As soon as the ramp is finished. Mom and Richard rush out to their romantic dinner together.

At least the boys are busy stuffing themselves with pizza. I can ignore them, dig in the top drawer of Mom's dresser where I know she's hidden my phone, and then shut myself in my room.

I knew it! There's a message from Asha!

Dear Superfan,
Thank you for visiting AshaJamil.com! I'm thrilled that you stopped by. Did you know that I recently released a new book? It's called *How to Save the Planet*. I know you'll love it! I'm on tour right now, so I can't respond personally to your message. Please pick up a copy of my new release and follow my adventures on YouHappy!
Kisses,
Asha Jamil

As I read, the hope dribbles out of me.

Of course, Asha doesn't respond personally to her messages. She probably gets thousands of them every day.

I turn my phone off and drag myself back to Mom's room, where I tuck it into place in the top drawer.

Downstairs, Ocean and Jackson are hollering at their screens.

"Ah! He exploded," Ocean yells.

Then, "I am respawning!"

"I'll come back to spawn," Jackson says.

I close my bedroom door, grab my notebook, and list all the ways Mom is stunting my future. Then I start a second list: all the ways Simone has misunderstood my commitment to fighting climate change.

My dedication to climate action is completely sincere. Obviously. Entirely. It's not as if I want the Earth to go up in smoke.

It was NOT my fault that I've been secretly eating meat. I've been doing it so I don't hurt Richard's feelings or Amelie's feelings.

How could Simone replace me on the podcast without even consulting me? And if I was a little, teensy bit furious that Amelie was going to interview Asha Jamil instead of me, I think that's entirely reasonable.

Growling, I toss my journal aside. It's not helping. The more things I add to my list, the angrier I get.

There's one of Mom's posters that used to hang in the living room of our apartment but now hangs in our upstairs hall above the computer. It shows a dark mountain range with the sun just peeking over the summit. The words read: "It's always darkest before the dawn." Not that I'm taking advice from my misguided mother these days, but I could really use some dawn soon. Something has to start going well. Maybe a sparkling new opportunity is right around the corner.

I try to think of what that might be.

It's difficult to concentrate over the sound of zombies. Ocean and Jackson have cranked the volume on their video game. When Mom and Richard left, they said the boys could play for an hour as long as they acted like civilized human beings. This is not civilized.

But at least they're occupied.

I'll simply shut them from my mind.

The climate march. I can still go. I'm signed up to volunteer, and Mya really needs people. Mr. Lau will probably be so busy with Asha's visit that he won't notice I'm missing.

Maybe Mya will have an emergency, and she'll need a youth leader to step up to the microphone in front of the crowd.

I'm dedicated to leading our school and our community toward a sustainable future. There's a lot we can do, even as students! From small things, like saving water, to big things, like letter-writing campaigns.

Downstairs, something scrapes across the floor.

"Everything okay?" I yell.

"Just bumped the coffee table. We're fine!" Ocean yells back.

I can't believe Mom thought this would be bonding time.

I know this city is full of smart, committed people. If we work together, we can do amazing . . .

Maybe my speech would get recorded, and then go viral.

"Jackson, heads up!" Ocean hollers.

"Oh, man!" Jackson is just as loud.

That's it. I climb off my bed and stomp downstairs to see what's happening.

It's a disaster.

There are candy wrappers everywhere. Fruit gummies are sprayed like confetti across the carpet. Jackson has a Halloween-level pile of chocolate in his lap and Ocean is jumping on the couch. The lamp — the one Mom and Richard bought together — is lying on its side across the rug.

"Ocean, what are you —"

He turns at my voice. He has a piece of red licorice shoved up each nostril. He looks like a crazed, jumping walrus.

"WHAT ARE YOU DOING?"

Jackson is laughing so hard he doesn't seem capable of speech. A chocolate smear extends from his ear to the corner of his mouth.

"Seriously," I say. "What is happening? Where did you get all this stuff?"

Ocean's jumping dislodges one of his licorice tusks and he dives after it. He lands on the coffee table, then rolls to the carpet, clutching one elbow. I can't tell if he's laughing or crying.

"Loser!" Jackson has regained the power of speech, apparently.

"Okay, stop." I stand in the middle of the room with my arms out like a traffic cop. Someone has to be the grown-up.

"Barbecue chips?" Jackson offers, holding out a bag.

For a brief moment, I'm tempted. Handling all this stress would be easier with barbecue chips to chew on instead of my nails. But . . .

"Really, where did you get this stuff?"

"We went to the store." Ocean's still holding his elbow. He's still lying on the floor. But at least the licorice is gone and his airways are clear.

"When? When did you go to the store?"

I know I haven't been paying the most attention, but I'm sure I heard them down here the whole time.

"When Dad said I could go and get Jackson."

"He said you could go to the store? By yourselves?"

"Well . . ." Ocean says.

"But my mom would have said yes," Jackson says.

"*Would* have said yes?"

He nods firmly.

"You didn't ask her."

"Peach gummies?" he offers. He seems to be picking the crescent-shaped candies from a mixed bag.

"Are you trying to give me the ones you don't like?"

He glances at Ocean and shrugs. They crack up.

I've run entirely out of patience. I point to the floor. "Ocean, clean up these wrappers before Mom and Richard get home. Jackson, get rid of that mountain of sugar in your lap."

I see his hand move just in time. "NOT by eating it!"

I'm trying to figure out if I'm going to be blamed for this.

Best to at least threaten them, I decide. "I'm telling your dad about all of this, Ocean. And your parents, too, Jackson."

That finally wipes the smiles from their faces, though not the streaks of chocolate.

"Seriously, you can have tons of this." Jackson holds up an entire handful of candy. "Pick whatever you'd like."

"How did you pay for it?" I spin around to glare at my pseudo-brother. "If you took money from my mom's purse, Ocean, you're going to be in HUGE trouble."

"It wasn't from her purse!" he protests.

Jackson makes frantic shushing sounds, but he's not fast enough. I step closer to Ocean and give him my best stare.

"It's money from our lemonade stand," he blurts.

"Lemonade stand," I say flatly.

He nods.

"The lemonade stand money you raised for charity?"

Suddenly, he seems very interested in gathering the candy wrappers from the floor.

"Well, we didn't tell people it was for charity, exactly," Jackson says.

"What? Ocean said —"

"We told people it was for kids with disabilities." He looks up at me. I swear he actually bats his lashes. "And I'm a kid with a disability."

Ocean has turned away from me, but I hear him snort. Then the candy wrappers go flying again, as he and Jackson disintegrate into uncontrolled giggles.

My brain explodes.

I take three deep breaths. Then three more.

I speak firmly and slowly over the mayhem. "Clean. This. Up. Before my mom and Richard get home. Or you are going to be in trouble forever."

There will be no more blackmail in my future. The moment Ocean mentions the word "bidet," I'll go straight to Mom with his history of lemonade-stand fraud. I would call her right this instant . . . if I were speaking to her.

"You stink and you ruin everything and no one likes you," Ocean yells after me as I stomp up the stairs.

"Clean up the candy!" I yell back.

I slam my door, open it, and slam it again for emphasis.

Then I sit on my bed and cry, for reasons unrelated to the candy disaster.

Because as I was walking up the stairs, I was already planning to text Simone and tell her the whole story. She would laugh until her stomach hurt. But I can't text her because I'm not supposed to use my phone and Simone thinks I'm a fraud and — here's the worst part — Ocean's entirely right.

I do ruin everything, and no one likes me.

It's possible that I'll miss the Asha Jamil visit, lose my friends, and march for the climate all by myself.

23

Getting Confrontational

At the hotel on Sunday morning, I dip my finger into the whipped cream on my white chocolate mocha. Not what Emily Post would recommend.

One of the baristas grins at me. "Have you heard we got a new bubble tea machine? We haven't put bubble tea on the menu yet, because we're still experimenting, but I can get you a sample if you'd like."

"Bubble tea! How exciting!" Mom says.

"I'd recommend the taro, personally," the barista says.

But I shake my head. I'm not in a bubble tea mood.

"Are you okay, sweetheart?" Mom asks as we leave the café.

I shrug.

"This isn't still about your phone, is it? I wanted to talk to you about that, but not if you're sulking."

"I'm not sulking."

It's difficult to say that sentence without sounding as if one is sulking.

Mom purses her lips. "Richard and I discussed this. You can have your phone back in a week, but there'll be no posting on YouHappy for a month."

"A month!?" My jaw practically drops to the floor.

"And if I see any more selfies on there before high school, that will become a year."

What? A year!?

"Agreed?"

I nod glumly. "Agreed."

Another week without my phone. It already feels like one of my arms is missing.

I trail Mom to the elevators, where she scans her security card. On the fourth floor, I follow her down the plush, carpeted hall and drop into my usual spot in her office.

"Homework this morning?" she asks, as she settles herself at her computer.

To answer, I hold up my math workbook. But when I open it, the numbers swim on the page. Math seems useless. Everything seems useless. Mr. Lau is single-handedly destroying the Earth and tricking everyone at Cedarview by using Asha, and there's not a single thing I can do about it. I can't text Simone. I can't post podcast stories. I can't use social media to contact anyone. By the time a month has passed, even @Texan5589567 will be bored with my account.

I have zero influence.

I stare at my workbook for a little longer, but nothing changes. I need something to make me feel better. Something . . . like the smell of fresh sheets.

"Can I go say hi to Janina?"

When Mom nods absently, I borrow her security card, let myself out of her office, and pad back to the elevators. As soon as I arrive on the sub-basement level, a damp heat and the scent of detergent wash over me. But Janina's not in her usual spot by the washing machines. I find her down the hall, opening plastic packages.

"What's that?" I ask, once she's finished kissing my cheeks.

She rolls her eyes. "Silk pillowcases," she says. "Some VIP guest this week, she sleeps only on silk. She says silk, so we buy silk."

She glances up at me. "What? You like silk?"

I've stopped breathing.

"Janina, do you know the name of your VIP guest?"

She shrugs. "No one tells me. Only that we need silk this, silk that. Oh, and coconut shampoo. Coconut only, they say."

She looks pleasantly surprised when I hug her. Then I set off in search of Howard, the security manager. My head is swirling. Could this be real?

"Good morning, Howard!"

His office is tucked behind the concierge desk. When I was small, I used to love coming in here and watching the lobby and the hallways through the lenses of the security cameras. Even now, it feels as if I've stepped into a spy movie.

"Emily!" He grins. "Hey, Peanut. Did you bring me any pancakes from the café?"

"Sorry. No leftovers."

I give him a wide smile and start asking questions about his work. Subtle questions.

"It must be tricky, balancing the security needs of all these important guests. Last week, Mom and I saw an opera singer in the elevator."

"That's nothing," he scoffs. "Some of these stars, they're such big deals they travel with their own teams. Then I get other people crammed in here with me, checking out the system."

"Someone like . . . say . . . a major TV star. Would they travel with security?"

"If they're a big deal, probably at least one security person, sure."

One security person, plus Howard.

"Do you have stars arriving every week?"

He nods. "Almost always. In just a few days, we've got someone big coming."

"And does this person have specific security needs?"

He snorts. "Peanut, you wouldn't believe the list of demands she sent. A room for her bodyguard. Silk sheets. A dog bed."

I refrain from squealing. Barely.

"Wow. What you do is really impressive, Howard."

"Let's hope she thinks so."

"If it's who I think it is . . . say, Asha Jamil?"

He raises an eyebrow. "You know I can't give out guest names, Peanut."

"Well, she's going to think you're fabulous. I'll see you soon!"

I give him a grin and a wave before he can ask any questions. I really do feel like a spy. As I retrace my steps to

Mom's office, I'm vibrating with possibilities. What if it's really Asha? Could I be wrong? No, I'm definitely right. Asha's staying at this exact hotel. In less than one week.

This exact hotel. Less than one week!

No matter how many times I try to tackle my math problems, those two points keep popping into my head.

After an hour or so, Mom glances up from her keyboard. "You've been busy," she says. "Did you get your homework done?"

I make a noncommittal sound. I've gotten a lot done. But none of it was homework.

It takes me two more days to finalize my plan. It would be faster if I had my phone, but I'm still restricted to obsolete communication forms.

I keep adding details, then crossing them out. Eventually, the third time I cross out the words "Prepare written apology in case things go wrong," I realize what I'm doing.

Procrastinating.

I march myself downstairs to the living room.

"Excuse me, Mom. Can we talk about the climate march?"

She looks up from the couch, where she's curled up with a magazine. She's opening her mouth to answer me when, with a shriek, Ocean barrels around the corner. He's wearing his undies and a bath towel, which billows behind him like a cape. It appears to be held in place by his chin. And tucked beneath his arm, Ocean carries . . .

"Is that my rooster?" Mom asks.

"ROAR!" Richard stomps into the room like a grizzly bear, arms above his head. "You cannot escape me!"

With another shriek, Ocean tries to duck between his legs.

"My rooster . . ." Mom says.

"ROAR!" Richard says.

And the rooster says . . . well, it says nothing. It lands on the floor, where it shatters into tiny pieces. Cookies fly in all directions.

Both Richard and Ocean freeze. They look at Mom with matching guilty expressions.

"My rooster . . ." Mom says again.

"Sorry," Richard says.

He nudges Ocean, who quickly apologizes.

I wait. Mom loves that rooster. I happen to know this because I bought it for her when I was in fourth grade, and she's told me multiple times how much she loves it. So I wait for her to explode. To cry. To rage.

She sighs, shaking her head. "I'll get the broom."

"MOM!"

Everyone freezes again. This time, they all look at me.

"Mom," I say, in a more reasonable tone. "You loved that rooster."

"I did, honey! It meant a lot to me, especially since you bought it for me."

"But it was kind of . . . ugly," Ocean says.

Richard's mouth quirks in what could be a fleeting smile.

I am officially appalled.

I know exactly what Emily Post would say about this. "Consideration for the rights and feelings of others is not merely a rule for behavior in public but the very foundation upon which social life is built." That's one of her most famous quotes.

I came downstairs to ask about the climate march, but now, climate change is forgotten in the face of a greater disaster. We live with monsters who have never even heard of common decency, let alone etiquette. And I'm tired of it.

"Mom, Ocean already wrecked your poster, and now he's smashed your rooster. He's so loud, we can't think. He leaves wet towels on the bathroom floor. He's running around the house practically naked. Richard SEXTS you. And there are inappropriate masks at our front door, waiting to scare anyone who visits!"

"What's sexting?" Ocean asks.

"You don't like the masks?" Richard asks at the same time.

"I HATE THE MASKS!" Not my most diplomatic moment. "AND YOU CAN'T BREAK THINGS THAT BELONG TO OTHER PEOPLE!"

Richard turns to Mom. "You don't like the masks?"

"Tell him the truth," I demand. Mom's never exactly told me she doesn't like the masks, but we've been mother and daughter for thirteen years. I *know*.

"The masks are . . . not my favorite," she admits.

"What's sexting?" Ocean asks.

"Later, bud," Richard says.

Mom turns to me. "Emily, this is an adjustment for all of us. We need to be flexible and —"

"Mom, we're the only ones being flexible!"

"Well, Ocean's only eight," she says.

"Ocean's old enough to steal charity money and buy himself candy!"

"Emily sprayed herself with the bidet!" Ocean blurts, but it's too late.

"He did what?" Richard asks. His voice is suddenly less fake-grizzly and more real.

The whole story comes out. The lemonade stand, the secret trip to the corner store, and the candy jamboree while Mom and Richard were out on their date.

"I didn't —" Ocean tries to interrupt.

Richard shoots him a look.

"It wasn't —"

"Not another word," Richard growls. It appears he's capable of discipline after all. In rare occurrences.

Once the two of them have marched next door to speak with Jackson and his parents, Mom pulls me down on the couch beside her.

"Why didn't you tell us sooner?"

"You would have taken Ocean's side. You take their side about everything. We're always so polite, they trample us."

For a few minutes, Mom doesn't say anything. I wait for her to start making excuses.

"That's not how I want you to feel," she says eventually.

Which doesn't sound like an excuse.

"And I have to admit, I really, really dislike those masks in the strongest possible terms."

"The strongest possible term is 'hate,' Mom."

"I hate the masks!"

She blurts it, then claps a hand over her mouth. I burst out laughing. I can't help it.

We talk for a few more minutes about how our townhouse life might feel a bit more balanced. Then I grab the broom and help sweep up the remains of the rooster.

"It *was* kind of ugly," I admit. "And loud."

"Sometimes we learn to love things that are loud," Mom says.

I roll my eyes.

"Too soon?"

"Too soon."

She suggests I head upstairs and enjoy some quiet time before Ocean and Richard return. But just before I leave, I remember the original issue.

"I need to go to the climate march on Friday."

"Oh, Richard and I meant to talk to you about that. After you mentioned it, we both took the day off. We'll all go together."

This is not ideal. But there are certain times when the only polite response is, "Um . . . great."

And maybe this is an opportunity.

"Mom?"

"Yes, sweetheart?"

"I know you said another week, but do you think I could have my phone back? I promise not to post any more pictures."

There's a long pause, and then she turns around and heads upstairs.

I hold my breath.

MY PHONE! SHE RETURNS WITH MY PHONE!

"I'm trusting you to be more responsible."

"I promise," I say.

My phone. Back in my hands.

Ocean should have broken that cookie jar a long time ago.

24

Powers of Persuasion

Wednesday is the official release day for October's *Cedarview Speaks* episode. Created by everyone except me.

First thing on Wednesday morning, I go in search of Simone and find her crammed into the podcast studio with Amelie, Daniella, and Reza. I only notice for a brief second that Amelie is spinning in *my* chair. Then I straighten my shoulders.

"Simone, can I talk to you?"

"Sorry, we're busy planning November," Simone says.

"Did you listen to today's episode?"

Their big story about missing permission slips? No.

"And we're writing our questions for the Asha Jamil interview," Amelie adds.

She and Simone simultaneously flip their hair.

This might kill me.

I step inside the studio and close the door behind me. Without the light from the library, the room is dim and claustrophobic.

"This seems . . . ominous," Reza says. Using a much bigger word than I would have thought possible.

"Emily! There's not enough room in here," Simone protests.

Daniella continues to stare at the computer, where the screen is filled with coding gibberish.

"You know how I said that Mr. Lau scheduled Asha's visit for the same afternoon as the climate march — on purpose?" I ask.

Amelie's eyes go wide. "Seriously? Why?"

So Simone didn't tell her. Interesting.

"He's doing it to keep us in the school, obviously!"

I shouldn't have added the "obviously." I remind myself that I need to convince Simone, and I try again in a nicer voice.

"Mr. Lau doesn't want us at the climate march because he doesn't want to offend CA Energy. He's basically sold out to —"

"CA Energy has 90 percent of its assets invested in traditional oil and gas," Daniella whispers, glancing up from her screen. "Despite its green initiatives campaign."

"That's horrible!" Amelie says.

Simone shakes her head. "It has nothing to do with this. And of course I want to go to the march. But . . . Asha. We can't miss the opportunity to meet her," Simone says.

"Asha posts all the time about climate change. She wouldn't —" Amelie says.

"She doesn't know," I interrupt. "But I think we should tell her."

Reza makes some sort of hooting sound. I can't tell if he's impressed or he thinks I'm bananas.

Simone sniffs. "Emily, no offence, but you've already caused a lot of trouble lately."

I've caused trouble? She's the one who yelled at me in the bathroom, and basically stole the podcast, and . . .

Argh. If I'm going to make my plan work, I really need her help.

"Simone, I'm sorry. I wasn't thinking about your feelings. And Amelie, I haven't been taking the vegan club seriously enough."

I stop, tugging at a stray strand of my hair. I guess I may as well come clean entirely . . .

"And it was my fault your posters got wrecked."

Now all three of them stare at me.

With a sigh, I spill the whole story. "I was just so mad, and then I did the first one, and I didn't mean for Marcus to —"

"Why were you mad again?" Amelie tilts her head to one side.

"Because you were . . . carrying the beakers?"

She looks completely confused.

"I know! It doesn't make sense. But you were hanging out with Simone, and then Simone was wearing yellow scarves and speaking French. And Ms. Flores loves you, and I got . . . jealous."

The word tastes like sour milk in my mouth.

"Emily Post says that jealousy is the suspicion of one's own inferiority." I want to race from the studio and bury my head in a beanbag chair. I have to force myself to continue. "And you're kind of impressive. And intimidating."

I wait for her to yell at me. But, after a second, the corner of her mouth twitches. "FART OF LIFE was pretty funny," she says.

"It was," Reza agrees.

Simone gasps. "Amelie, you worked hard on those posters. And that was so rude!" She glares at me.

"I know!" I say. "I've been horrible and I'm sorry."

"Really sorry, or sorry because you need our help?" Simone narrows her eyes.

Well, that's a tricky one.

"Both," I say eventually.

They listen carefully as I lay out my plan.

"And this way, you'll still get to meet Asha," I tell Simone.

Daniella seems to be hyperventilating in the corner.

"Are you okay?" I ask.

"I have a lot to do," she whispers. "I have to go."

"Do you need help?" Amelie asks, her forehead creased.

"I'm fine. See you in a bit."

Squeezing past the other three in their spinning chairs, then past me at the door, she makes her escape.

"Did you hear she talked to Ms. Flores about Bryce?" Simone whispers, once Daniella's gone.

"She did?" I gasp.

"Bryce is off the basketball team and he has to help out in the cafeteria for a month," Reza says glumly.

We all stare at him.

"Okay, he deserved it," Reza admits.

I look back to Simone. "What about the Asha thing? Can you help?"

"You don't even know for sure if she's staying at The Allegra. There are other people who like silk sheets and coconut shampoo."

I raise my eyebrows. Amelie raises hers.

"I'm sure there are other people . . ." Simone's voice trails off. Because she knows I'm right.

"Wait a second . . . the two of you aren't planning to do this alone, right? I definitely want in," Reza says.

I stare at him.

"Yeah, I'm coming, too," Amelie says.

"But we'll —" I start.

"You can't expect us to hang out at school while you get to meet Asha in person," Amelie says. "Besides, you wrecked my posters. You owe me." She softens the words with a smile.

I hold out another minute, but then I shrug. It might actually be easier to do this with four of us.

"So, what do you think of the plan?" I ask.

They have a few suggestions.

We spend half of math class working out the details. (Thankfully, Mr. Gill has a sub today, and the sub loses all control within the first ten minutes.)

Our revised plan would be easier with five people, but Daniella refuses to help. When I try to talk to her in the hallway between classes, she says she's swamped with a different project. Because she looks as if she might pass out at any moment, I don't pressure her.

Reza, meanwhile, seems to think this is the best week of his life.

"I wish we had access to a helicopter," he says, sliding into the desk beside mine in English.

"What?"

"You know, one that would fly down and lift us from the top of the hotel, right at the climactic moment. When it looks as if all is lost. We're going to die. Then . . . thwump, thwump, thwump . . . the chopper arrives."

"Reza, no one is going to die. And there will be no helicopters," I say.

Is it really necessary to take him with us? I run through the plan in my head one more time and, unfortunately, it is. We're already going to be rushed because Daniella won't help.

"I bet you'd make a great helicopter pilot," Reza says.

Well, that's sort of nice. "I'm sure you'd be a good pilot too," I say.

He looks ridiculously pleased with himself.

Thursday finally arrives. It's go time. Simone, Amelie, Reza, and I spend the end of lunch hour and the first ten minutes of social studies shut inside the old downstairs locker room, where Marcus promised no one would find us. (I feel bad risking one of his hiding spots, but he said it was fine when he heard we might save the Earth.) Everyone else is dressed normally, but I have a ball cap pulled tightly over my frizzy hair.

Once the hallways are empty, we scoot from the locker room, across the hall, and out the side doors of the school. Then, as if we have nothing to hide, we stroll across the grass field and out the far gate. The whole time, I wait for a voice to stop us. I wait for someone to ask what exactly we think we're doing. But five minutes later we're on the sidewalk walking toward the bus stop, and we're . . . free.

"Step one, *fait accompli!*" Simone says.

I have to remind myself to breathe. Somehow, Simone and Amelie manage to smile at the bus driver and pay our fares. They stand in the aisle of the bus, chit-chatting with Reza the entire way downtown, while I sit on a bench seat like a frozen popsicle.

"Emily, are you okay? We don't have to do this if you've changed your mind," Amelie says.

I don't know if I'm okay.

"Are *you* okay? Are you sure *you* want to do this?" I ask her.

I've dragged her into it. And even if she's occasionally annoying, she seems like a basically nice person.

"What if we all get expelled forever and you have to go back to Lake Pointe West?" I ask.

"We're not going to get expelled, *mes amies*," Simone says. But Amelie looks uncomfortable.

"Seriously, you can wait here, and we can meet you after," I tell her. We'll have to go back to my original plan, and our chances won't be great, but I can't force someone else into a criminal lifestyle.

"It's not that," she says.

We wait, though Simone bounces on her tiptoes.

"I never went to Lake Pointe West," Amelie says. "I don't have that much money. Hardly any money, actually."

Simone gasps. "*C'est impossible!*"

"How . . . what about your earrings?" I say. Which I realize makes sense to no one except me.

"My dad bought my earrings."

Okay, maybe it made sense to Amelie.

"I live with my mom. Until last year, I was homeschooled. But I really, really wanted to go to a regular school. And when my mom finally agreed, I didn't want to be weird. The vegan thing was already weird enough, and —"

"Whoa. How did you get your mom to agree?" Reza asks.

"She didn't have time to homeschool me anymore. She started a food truck."

"THE TEMPEH MOBILE!" I exclaim.

Everyone on the bus turns to stare.

"Sorry. I saw The Tempeh Mobile at the auditorium announcement. That's your mom's food truck?" I ask, at a regular volume.

"What's tempeh?" Reza asks.

"It's made out of fermented soybeans," Amelie says. "It's kind of —"

"Gross," Simone says. Then she claps a hand over her mouth.

"Wait. Did you know about all of this?" I glare at her.

"No! I just tried some of the tempeh from Amelie's lunch, and it was disgusting."

It's not exactly polite to call someone else's food disgusting. But it does make me love Simone a little bit more.

"That wasn't tempeh. That was a soytein patty," Amelie says.

"Dude, you're like a secret agent or something," Reza says, looking at Amelie admiringly.

"Or something," I say wryly. I'd hardly call Amelie a secret agent.

Somehow, Amelie's revelation has helped my brain get back in gear. I can think again. And it's time to review our final details.

"Thanks for telling us, Amelie," I say.

"We don't care how much money you have," Simone says.

"Or that you're an undercover vegan operative," Reza adds.

This is getting ridiculous.

"Reza, I need you to focus on me."

Oops, that didn't sound quite right.

"I mean, because this is almost our stop. We get off this bus in two more minutes, and then it's stage two of our plan."

"What was stage one?" Simone asks.

"Getting out of the school."

"How many stages are there?"

I suddenly have new respect for secret agents, vegan or otherwise.

25

Emily ~~Post Laurence~~ Bond

The plan is not complicated. Simone and I are going to wait at the back door of The Allegra, near the elevators. This way, none of the staff will recognize me in the lobby. Reza and Amelie are going to take the main doors into the hotel. Once they're inside, they'll split up. Reza will pretend he's heading for the elevators, but he'll really unlock the service door for Simone and me. Meanwhile, Amelie will head for Howard's office behind the concierge desk and try to distract him. As soon as Simone and I are inside, Reza will double back to help Amelie.

That's the plan. But Simone and I have been standing in the alley behind the hotel for five minutes already, and Reza hasn't turned up.

Simone is staring at her phone screen, and she doesn't seem to notice the delay.

"Have you seen this?" she asks, her voice a little awestruck.

"I'm really not in the mood to admire Asha's outfits right now," I tell her.

"No . . . this!" She holds her phone beneath my nose, and I have to step back so my eyes can focus.

Help beta test our new product: BullyBuster! An app that will let you report bullies, if you choose, or ask for support from your fellow students. Click below to learn more!

"BullyBuster?" I repeat.

"Daniella made an app!" Simone looks as if she's about to burst with pride.

"Did you know about this?"

And where is Reza? Why are we stuck in the alley? This plan can't possibly go awry before it even starts.

"I only knew she was working on it."

"It's seriously impressive." I had no idea Daniella was capable of such . . . action.

"She didn't tell me what she was going to call it, obviously," Simone says. "I never would have let her choose BullyBuster."

"The name's a disaster," I agree. "As is our current predicament."

I bounce on my toes, staring at the door as if that will make it open. But I am, somewhere in the back of my brain where I can process un-Asha-related thoughts, entirely impressed with Daniella.

"Shouldn't Reza be here by now?" Simone asks.

And then, finally, the back door clicks open.

"What took you so long?" I hiss.

"It's been about thirty seconds," Reza says. "Did you want me to sprint across the lobby?"

I glare at him.

"Okay, I ate an oatmeal cookie. They were handing them

out in the lobby. And it would have looked suspicious if I'd walked right past a free sample."

I take a deep breath. "Can you just hurry to the security desk? We can't have Howard watching those cameras, or he'll see us."

"I'm on it," he says, pulling his basketball from his backpack. "I was born to create distractions."

Simone's nails dig into my arm as we step into the brass elevator. I stole Mom's security card from her purse. This probably caused problems for Mom this morning, but she'll hopefully forgive me when I explain why it was necessary. For now, I hold the card to the elevator panel and press the button for the top floor. The doors slide closed.

This might actually work. We might do it.

We step off the elevator and I lead Simone toward the corner suite. That's the fanciest one in the hotel, and I'm sure Asha will be there. The hotel is built like a box, with hallways in a tight square around the central elevators, and the guest rooms on the outsides. We turn right into the hall and . . .

I slam straight into a brick wall. Or . . . wait. Once I step back, I can see I really hit the wide chest of Howard, in his security uniform. I guess he's not downstairs at his desk.

I don't recognize the suit-wearing man beside him. He looks like a bodyguard right out of the movies, complete with a brush-cut and an earpiece.

I quickly pull my ball cap tighter on my head.

"Are you staying at the hotel, girls?" the stranger asks. His deep voice seems to echo down the hallway.

"Room 948," Simone blurts.

I roll my eyes. There is no such thing as a room 948. The Allegra has only eight rooms per floor, and only four on the penthouse level.

I tilt back the brim of my hat. "Howard, it's me. Susan's daughter?"

He breaks into a wide grin. "Hey, it *is* you! What are you doing here, Peanut?"

"Peanut?" Simone murmurs.

At least my nickname is vegan.

My brain is babbling. *Stop babbling.*

"We popped in to visit my mom."

Howard looks doubtful. "We've got strict orders this week. No one on this floor except registered guests. And you know your mom doesn't work up here."

"Fourth floor," I say, eyes as wide as I can make them.

"This is the fourteenth floor, Peanut."

"What?! I must have pressed the wrong button in the elevator!"

I decide a forehead slap would be too melodramatic.

"Are we on the wrong floor?" Simone echoes. Without even glancing at her, I know her eyes will be wider than mine. "Emily, you're such a dunce!"

Howard stares at us for a minute. He seems unconvinced.

"Tell you what," he says, finally. "We'll escort your friend to the lobby. And I'll radio your mom and tell her you're on your way to her office. On the *fourth* floor."

"Great!"

Simone's right. I'm a dunce. A complete dunce.

Howard leads the way back to the elevators. As the door slides open, he ushers us in. First Simone, then me, then the unknown security guard. Only Howard remains on the fourteenth floor as the doors give a faint beep and slide closed on all our climate-saving hopes. How could our plan fall apart so quickly?

Silently, we watch the numbers scroll past.

Seventh floor. Sixth. Fifth.

"So, do you enjoy your job?" Simone chirps.

The security guard stares down at her.

At the fourth floor, the doors slide open and I step out, turning back toward Simone with what I hope looks like the innocent smile of a girl who's never even dreamed of breaking a rule.

"See you in the lobby in a few minutes," I say.

Simone's at the very back of the elevator, behind the guard. She points dramatically to the ceiling.

"GO BACK UP," she mouths.

I don't change my fake grin and I don't roll my eyes. These are the two biggest accomplishments of the day so far. Emily Post would be proud of me.

"Directly to your mom's office," the guard says as the doors slide closed again.

I nod, as if I would never consider anything else. And I wouldn't, if the world weren't going to end due to forest fires, floods, and other climate-related disasters.

As soon as the elevator has gone, I press the button again. And pray.

Thankfully, the other elevator opens almost immediately. It's empty.

This time, I definitely hold my breath all the way to the fourteenth floor.

When the doors open, I peek out. I look up and down the hallway.

No Howard.

Silently, I pad to the right and round the first corner. The hallway is still clear. Then, just as I'm about to round the second corner, I hear the crackle of a radio.

"Yeah, boss?"

Howard is only a few steps away! I back up, slowly, holding my breath.

"Room service? Right. I'll meet the elevator."

I turn and scurry, as quietly as I can. Thank goodness for plush carpets. I race back along the hall, around the corner, past the elevators, and around the square in the opposite direction. I glance behind me.

No Howard.

And there it is: Room 1404.

I take a second to catch my breath and smooth my hair. Then I raise my hand to knock.

And stop.

What if she opens the door? What am I going to say to Asha Jamil? What if I can't say anything and I stand there, mouth gaping, until Howard returns? He'll probably arrest me. Can security guards make arrests? What if my mom has to bail me out of jail?

Wait . . . what if Asha *doesn't* open the door? What if I was wrong about the silk sheets and coconut shampoo, and some aging rock star with sensitive skin opens the door?

I could probably get back downstairs without anyone seeing me. I could find Amelie and Simone in the lobby. I could tell them I got caught again.

If I do that, Asha Jamil will spend tomorrow talking to the whole school while the climate march happens a few blocks away.

I knock.

My heart is beating so quickly, I see spots for a minute. I put a hand on the doorframe so Asha Jamil doesn't find a puddle of me lying across her threshold.

But it's not Asha who answers.

It's not an aging rock star, either.

It's the CA Energy guy, Chris Campbell, with his tufty ginger hair and his glasses. What is *he* doing here?

He barely glances at me.

"Sorry, sweetheart. Ms. Jamil is not giving autographs today."

A poodle — Asha's poodle! — tries to leap past him, its tongue lolling, but Mr. Campbell blocks it with his foot and pushes it away.

I put my hand on the door as he starts to swing it closed. "It's not . . . I'm not . . ."

I knew this would happen. I'm only managing to stammer.

Then Asha appears behind Mr. Campbell, scooping Lumpkin into her arms.

Asha Jamil.

The Asha Jamil.

TV star and pretend astronaut Asha Jamil.

I lose even the ability to stammer. It's really her!

She's gorgeous. But she's also . . . normal. She's wearing pink sweatpants and a black tank top and she's not much taller than I am. Her hair is damp and she wears a towel across her shoulders.

"Chris, don't scare her," she says.

She looks at me expectantly.

My legs are shaking so badly, I have to keep my hand on the doorframe. "I'm here to do an interview for *Cedarview Speaks*, the podcast of Cedarview Middle School," I blurt.

"I thought that was tomorrow," Asha says.

Mr. Campbell is already shaking his head. "Ms. Jamil is fully committed today. Why don't I give you my card, and we can schedule something?"

As he fishes in the pocket of his suit jacket, my heart sinks.

Asha peers past me into the empty hallway.

"You're not taking photos, right?"

I shake my head, not daring to hope. "No photos. It's a podcast."

She sets Lumpkin down, then turns and tosses the towel onto the floor of the hotel bathroom. I feel a momentary pang of sympathy for the housekeeping staff. It's a disaster in there already. But who cares about towels if —

"Just let her stay, Chrissy. She can interview me while I do my makeup." She grins over her shoulder at me. "I'll give you some makeup tips as we go!"

"That would be so great!" My voice squeaks. I really need to calm down.

"Asha," Chris says, in the same tone Richard uses when Ocean's being unreasonable.

"I mean, you're already here an hour early, right, Chris?" Asha says.

Is there a hint of tension between them?

"My friends are in the lobby," I blurt. "They have our recording equipment. Could they join us?"

"Absolutely not," Mr. Campbell says.

"Chris, are you in charge of protecting me now? From kids?" Asha asks. And her voice is perfectly polite but there's an edge of something in it. Something a little icy.

"I'm only here in case you need anything," he says.

"Right. That's what I thought." Asha turns to me and grins. "I was late for one appearance last week — one! — because I had a serious bubble tea craving. Do you like bubble tea?" She doesn't wait for my nod. "Anyway, one late appearance, and now I have a babysitter."

"I'm not a babysitter," Mr. Campbell protests. "I'm simply here to —"

"Make sure I don't need anything, I know." That crackle of ice again.

Lumpkin sits at her feet and whines softly.

Asha grabs the phone from the glass-topped desk and hits a button. "Yes. I have friends waiting in the lobby. Some young fans. I was wondering if you could . . ." She pauses, glancing at me. "How many?"

"Three," I say. I may regret inviting Reza into this room, but he did help with the plan. It would be impolite to leave him out.

"Three," she repeats into the phone.

Once she hangs up, she raises one perfectly groomed eyebrow. "Chrissy, you know what we're going to need? Bubble tea."

"I don't think they offer bubble tea at The Allegra, Asha."

The reality of the situation strikes me. Asha Jamil wants bubble tea. And I'm standing in her hotel room, knowing exactly where she can get it.

"Actually, the Opus Café downstairs is just experimenting with a new bubble tea machine. It's not on the menu yet, but —"

"See, Chrissy? There's a place just downstairs! Be a dear and get one mango and . . ." She pauses, looking at me expectantly. "What would you and your friends like?"

"Taro?"

She claps her hands as if I've chosen perfectly. "Forget the mango, Chrissy. Five taro bubble teas with pearls. You're a sweetheart."

Ha! Now who's the sweetheart, Mr. Campbell?

And it's going to take forever to make FIVE bubble teas.

I try my best to keep my face blank, without an iota of gloating, but it's extremely, exponentially difficult.

Asha practically pushes Mr. Campbell from the room.

As the door swings closed behind him, the reality of this situation sinks in. I'm in a hotel room with Asha Jamil. And I'm talking. At least, I'm about to talk. And —

"Why don't you tell me about your podcast while we wait. And do you mind if I finish my makeup? Otherwise, I'll be late and . . . well . . . you saw how Chris feels about schedules."

She sinks gracefully onto the bench in front of her dresser, clicks open a portable makeup mirror, and begins applying mascara. Lumpkin curls at her feet.

My mind goes blank.

After a second, Asha glances over at me. I expect her to look irritated, but she doesn't. She puts her mascara wand down on the desk (another mess for housekeeping to clean), then she steps toward me and grabs my hand.

"Deep breath," she says.

I obey. What is happening right now, exactly?

"Did you know I used to have the most horrible stage fright?"

That can't possibly be true. I shake my head.

"I was always worried about saying the wrong thing and offending someone. But I realized, eventually, that I was stronger than my fear. I wanted things, and my stage fright didn't want me to have them. I wasn't going to let it win. Right?"

That makes a strange sort of sense.

"Picture the strongest person you know, and just BE that person."

I picture Emily Post. Influencer. Independent woman. During World War II, she helped bring Jewish orphans to safety in the United States. In 1950, she was named one of the most powerful women in the country. Emily Post would never stand here silently. She would have told Asha everything by now.

"You're THAT strong. You are never going to let the fear win," Asha says.

I'm an influencer. Just like Emily Post. I take another deep breath and nod at Asha. Who knew I came to her hotel room for counseling?

"Okay, now . . . go!"

And I do. I mean, I sound like a chipmunk, but at least words are forming.

"I'm interested in your views on climate change."

"Oh!" She sounds surprised. She probably expected me to ask about the weird, clear goo she's currently brushing onto her eyebrows. "Well, I'm fully in support of climate action. You know my mom's parents were from Bangladesh, right? And that place is going to be seriously underwater soon. We need to turn this planet around, quick."

Okay, this is perfect. Now I just need to phrase the next part so she doesn't kick me out of the room.

"So, your big sponsorship deal with CoastFresh and CA Energy . . ."

"I don't know a ton about the company, but they have this new green initiative? They're building these massively huge wind farms . . . I can't remember where. North, somewhere?"

"Right, but green initiatives like that are less than 10 percent of their business. They're still heavily investing in oil exploration."

Thank you, Daniella, for that information.

"Yikes. You can maybe ask Chris about that when he gets back?"

There's a knock at the door. Lumpkin barks expectantly.

"Could you grab that for me?" Asha asks.

When I open it, Simone and Reza burst in, their faces flushed. Reza gawks at the posh room, but Simone has eyes only for Asha.

"*Ma . . . ma cherie*," she stammers.

And Asha is polite enough to pretend she doesn't hear.

26

Meet the Press

Once she's met everyone, Asha puts her makeup away and settles herself on the couch. She motions to me and pats the cushion beside her. (I'm about to sit beside Asha Jamil! And Lumpkin is licking my feet!) Simone and Reza pull up rolling chairs.

"Where's Amelie?" I whisper, but Simone only shakes her head.

She pulls out her phone. "Is it okay if I record the rest of the interview for our podcast?" she asks.

Asha smooths her hair. "Of course," she says.

Simone nods to me. We might only have a few minutes to tell Asha about the climate march before someone like Howard barges in looking for me and . . .

"I've already told Asha that CA Energy is investing in a LOT of oil exploration." I nod at my best friend. "Maybe you can explain what's happening at our school?"

Simone's face lights up, as if I've given her unlimited access to New York Fashion Week. And, with a few additions from Reza, she manages to tell Asha about the climate march, Mr. Lau's strategic scheduling, and the school sponsorship deal.

"We don't want you to be used for something you might not agree with," I say, once Simone has finished.

"Goodness," Asha says. "This is, like, a lot."

We all nod.

"You know what I'd do?" Reza says.

I cringe. I really don't want to know what Reza would do. It probably involves throwing a basketball at someone's head.

"I'd ditch the school and speak at the climate march instead. We know the organizer." He looks at me. "We do, right?"

"We do," Simone says.

"Well, it's not quite that easy," Asha says. "I mean, Chris is going to —"

As if she's conjured him, I hear his voice in the hallway, along with the voice of . . . Howard? And . . .

"The principal and Mr. Campbell, they don't want students joining in the march and jeopardizing the sponsorship deal," I blurt, trying to be as persuasive as possible in my last moments on Earth. "But you value the environment, like we do —"

"Are you sure it's Emily? I can't believe she'd barge in like this."

That's my mom's voice.

"Asha, you're our only hope for fixing this situation," I say.

The hotel room door swings open.

"It seems we have a security breach, and these kids aren't supposed to be here," Mr. Campbell says. He's holding a tray of bubble tea, which takes away from his serious tone somewhat.

Simone and Reza pop up from their chairs and take a few nervous steps backwards.

I stay where I am on the couch, focusing on Asha.

"They're using you. To prevent climate action," I tell her.

"Emily!" I can't tell by Mom's tone whether she's going to ground me for life or she's just surprised to see me here.

"I think that's enough for today," Mr. Campbell says firmly.

He glances at Howard, who steps forward.

I move to join Simone and Reza, but I'm still looking at Asha.

"You're an amazing influencer. But you need to influence people to do good things. If you could tell our principal —"

"Let's go, young lady," Howard says.

He reaches for my arm, but Lumpkin suddenly lunges for him. The poodle gets a mouthful of his suit sleeve.

"I love that dog," Simone breathes.

While Howard's busy detaching the poodle, I step to the side.

Mom's still struggling to figure out what's happening. "Emily, this isn't —"

"Out, all of you," Mr. Campbell says.

"Wait!"

When Asha speaks, we all freeze. Maybe she has time-bending abilities. Maybe all celebrities do.

She looks at me. "Emily, you're sure that they intentionally booked me for tomorrow afternoon so that kids couldn't go to the climate march?"

I nod. "I'm positive."

"That's ridiculous," Mr. Campbell says. "CA Energy is supportive of youth initiatives."

"As long as they're completely under your control," I say.

"Emily!" Mom says again.

Asha nods. "Chris, why don't you and I have a little chat about this?"

"Asha, sweetheart, I can guarantee you CA Energy doesn't concern itself with student projects. This is ridiculous."

That's when Daniella wriggles between Mom's elbow and Howard's, appearing in the room like an extremely quiet superhero.

"Actually, it *is* ridiculous," she says.

Forget the quiet part. She puts some serious volume on those words. Mr. Campbell almost drops his tray of bubble tea. He sets it quickly on the dresser and spins toward her.

Daniella folds her arms across her chest.

"Dad, you totally planned this. I heard you talking to Mr. Lau on the phone."

"Daniella?" Mr. Campbell says.

"Dad?" Simone, Reza, and I say, in the same disbelieving tone. Did she just call Mr. Campbell her dad?

There are four adults staring at Daniella now, plus the three of us. But she doesn't seem to care. She plants her feet on the carpet and glares at Mr. Campbell.

"Dad, I learned a lot this week about standing up for what's right. And it's time for you to do that. What you and Mr. Lau arranged was just . . . wrong."

"I have to . . . my job . . ."

"You don't even like your job. You liked your old job at the ad agency so much better."

Before our eyes, Mr. Campbell deflates like a boba in a cup of day-old bubble tea.

"Well, it sounds like I might be joining a climate march," Asha says brightly.

Things go pretty well for our mini rebellion after that. Asha mentions something about lawyers and meetings. Howard returns to the hallway. Then Mom ushers the rest of us downstairs.

"Out of Ms. Jamil's hair," she says.

But Asha asks us not to leave the hotel just yet.

"I want to talk more," she says.

That sentence gives Reza just enough time to grab our tray of bubble teas. Considerately, he leaves one behind for Asha.

An hour later, we're downstairs in the Opus Café, watching as Mya, the march organizer, meets with Asha Jamil about her upcoming climate march appearance.

I'm 10 percent jealous of Mya, because she now seems to be Asha's best friend.

"I know!" she exclaims. "He called me 'sweetheart' too, at a media announcement. So patronizing!"

Asha touches her hand.

"She touched her hand!" Simone breathes.

I turn to Amelie. "I still can't believe you gave up your own chance to interview Asha so you could arrange this."

It turns out Amelie had the last-minute idea to call Mya. Simone gave her the number, and Amelie phoned and said it was a climate emergency. She stayed in the lobby to meet Mya.

Reza, Simone, Amelie, and I squeeze together at the next table over, watching the meeting, sipping a second round of bubble teas, and congratulating ourselves.

"We met Asha Jamil. We're sitting right now with Asha Jamil," Simone whispers into her cup.

Daniella has taken her dad home, apparently to think about his wrongdoings.

Once Mom heard the whole story — or at least what I could explain in five minutes, with a bunch of other people watching — she agreed to let me stay at the hotel for a while. She's waiting in her office.

"You did a good job upstairs," I tell Reza. It will probably make his head swell, but it's true.

"Team effort," he says.

"True." I smile at Amelie. "You did a good job downstairs."

She shrugs. "I didn't want CA Energy getting away with this. And I didn't just call Mya, I called —"

Before she finishes her sentence, a woman with long braids steps into the café. Amelie pops up from the table and greets her.

"Wait . . . is that . . ."

"Eternity Williams, from *West Side Community News*." Amelie introduces her.

"You're the woman who wrote the profile about Ocean!"

"Well, she writes important news, too," Simone says. "Amelie called *all* the newspapers."

I watch as Amelie leads the new arrival to Asha's table. The journalist sits beside Mya. Soon, all three of them are deep in conversation. I can hear the words "corporate sponsorship" and "youth-led action."

I don't even care that I'm sitting at a side table. I don't care that Mya, Asha, and Eternity are all using their influence to boost the climate march, without me. I'm so, so happy to be sipping bubble tea right now. Simone is speaking to me. Amelie is insisting they should all quit the podcast unless Mr. Chadwick reinstates me. And, under the table, Reza's foot is touching mine. It might be accidental and it might be on purpose, but either way, it's kind of . . . nice?

I can't believe I just thought that.

Twenty minutes later, the interview is wrapping up. Mom pokes her head into the café just in time.

"Anyone need a ride home?"

We chorus goodbye to Asha, who kisses each of us on the cheek. Reza turns eggplant purple and loses the ability to speak. Then he and Amelie decide to bus home. Simone, Mya, and I pile into Mom's car.

"That was amaZING!" Mya gushes, as soon as the doors close. "I can't believe I met Asha Jamil! Thank you both, really, for organizing this. You are fabulous. I hope you'll be joining the high-school journalism club next year, and of course the Climateers. We need people like you."

And just like that, *Cedarview Speaks* becomes a little less important. I'm going to be a serious journalist next year. I won't need middle-school influence anymore.

"Plus I'll see you at the climate march, right?" Mya asks. "You're going to volunteer?"

"We'll be there," I promise.

When we drop Mya off, I'm floating on a cloud of influential bliss. Until the door closes behind her.

Mom looks at Simone and me through her rear-view mirror.

"You two," she says, "have some explaining to do."

Fortunately, Simone and I are excellent at explaining. It's one of our most fabulous talents.

27

We March!

The march doesn't officially start for two hours, but the square in front of City Hall is already packed with people. Giant inflatable whales bob along one sidewalk, tethered to protesters dressed all in blue. I see a man on stilts, wearing a brilliant scarlet bird costume. There's another group holding seedlings toward the sky. In between are hundreds and hundreds of signs.

The dinosaurs thought they had time, too.
The world's already hotter than my boyfriend.
Things are so bad, even introverts are marching.

I hold my own sign high, with its drawing of Emily Post. In big, beautiful, Simone-drawn letters, it reads: "Be polite! Share the Earth!"

Simone says people won't recognize Emily Post, but I don't care. Emily helped get me here. It's only fair to let her see the march.

"Are you okay?" I ask Simone.

She has a death grip on my arm. And I have to shout

into her ear because the police are closing the intersections. A siren blares from one corner.

She nods. "Great!"

We make our way across the square, dodging pockets of people, until we reach the giant yellow media tent beside the stage. There, Mya's wielding a bullhorn in one hand and a clipboard in the other. Amelie waves at us.

"You made it! Perfect!" Mya calls.

I tuck my sign against the tent as she gives us our official volunteer badges and reels off a list of instructions. Only people with media lanyards are allowed in the tent. We have information sheets to hand out to journalists, and extra power banks if they need to charge their phones. The first-aid tent is next door.

"I'm off to check the sound system!" Mya shouts, rushing in the direction of the stage.

She has barely disappeared when Mom, Richard, and Ocean arrive. Richard balances Ocean on his shoulders, where Ocean holds a giant inflatable Earth. I see a lot of potential issues with this arrangement...

"Oh, thank goodness you made it safely on the bus," Mom breathes. "What a mob scene! Have you got your phone?" she asks. "Keep your ringer on at all times. We'll meet you here after the march."

"Mom, I'm fine."

Richard grins at me as he pulls her away. "C'mon, Susan. We have to save the Earth!"

They have to save two Earths, actually, because Ocean's inflatable bounces away over the heads of the crowd.

My family (my family!) takes off in pursuit.

The first half hour in the tent is easy, then there's a rush of journalists plugging in cameras and arranging microphones. I spot Eternity Williams, the newspaper reporter, in a daffodil-yellow jacket. There's a local news anchor, too, with a full crew trailing behind her.

"My mom's a big fan," I say as the anchor rushes by, but she doesn't hear me. She's busy directing her camera operator on the right angle for her shot. She looks like a regular person until the moment the camera turns on. Then she straightens her shoulders, dips her chin, and smiles.

"We're at City Hall, where today's climate march is about to begin. Organizers are expecting a crowd of several hundred young people."

She relaxes. "We'll get the next shot from over by that floating whale," she calls.

They're gone.

At exactly 10:00 a.m., there's a squeal of microphone feedback, then Mya begins speaking. Even though I'm near the stage, there are hundreds of people blocking the view. I can only see the top of her head. When Mya thanks everyone for coming out, the crowd's response is somewhere between a cheer and a roar.

"How many people turned up, do you think?" a fellow volunteer asks me.

A woman in front of us — a gray-haired woman with "Rebel Grandma" scrawled on her shirt — turns around. "They say at least a thousand!"

We stand at the edge of the tent for a few minutes as Mya's voice tells us about a CA Energy natural gas project approved without public consultation and without input from Indigenous groups. She says the Climateers are part of a larger group taking the government to court.

I stand on my tiptoes and crane my neck to see better, but part of my view is now blocked by the balloon whales.

"Are we still in charge of this tent?" Amelie asks. "I want to circle to the front."

I glance around. The few journalists using the tent seem to know what they're doing. We're not exactly useful.

"Go ahead," I say. "I can stay here."

On stage, an Indigenous man takes the microphone. He says the land where the natural gas project is being built was never ceded to the government. He says the local council has no authority to build and no public license.

There are more roars and more cheers after every sentence.

After a minute, Amelie struggles back toward me.

"Excuse me."

"Pardon me."

"Can I squeeze through?"

She turns sideways and slides through the last gap between elbows and shoulders.

"Whew! It is WILD out there!"

Another Climateer takes the microphone and begins a chant.

Hey hey, ho ho,
climate change has got to go.
Hey hey, ho ho,
climate change has got to go.

They're not the most sophisticated lyrics in the world, but the crowd amplifies her words a thousand times, until it seems as if the walls of City Hall are vibrating.

"And now," calls the Climateer, "we march!"

Mya said other volunteers would watch over the media tent once the crowd was moving, so I grab my sign and we follow the stream of people along the streets of downtown. The whole way, people with drums and bullhorns lead chants and bang drums. Some people write slogans on the walls of buildings using sidewalk chalk. And every once in a while, the whales bob into view. I even see an inflatable Earth, once.

I hold my phone high and snap a photo of the marchers, to show Marcus when I get back to school.

Climate action now!

I post the photo to my YouHappy account, too. (Technically, I'm still banned from social media for the month, but Mom gave me a one-day exemption.)

As of next week, I'll have even more posting to do. I'm a new member of the Climateers social media team! It's a high-school club, but I get to join early. It's going to take a lot of my time. I may even let Amelie permanently take my place on the podcast team so I can devote myself to my new, influential responsibilities.

I found some great Emily Post advice last night. She said that when you're hurt, you shouldn't nurse your bruises. You should get up and be courageous. Get ready for the next challenge. That's what I'm going to do.

Simone elbows me. "Stop walking and texting. You're going to trip."

"But look!" A dozen people have already liked my post. I'm building influence with every planet-saving step.

28

A Tempeh Buffet

I take a picture of Amelie and Simone hauling boxes of ingredients from The Tempeh Mobile.

Happening today: Cedarview's first vegan extravaganza! #PlantBasedLife

I post it to the Climateers account first, then like it from my own account. (I'm up to sixty-seven followers now!)

"Are you going to help or are you just going to watch?" Simone calls. Her arms look as if they might pull from their sockets. I tuck my phone away and rush to grab one end of her box.

"On the counter at the far side, girls," Ms. Lydia directs us as we enter the school cafeteria.

She has the place running like a military operation. The cafeteria workers are already frying tempeh patties under the watchful eye of Amelie's mom, a blonde in a pencil skirt and a white chef's jacket who looks nothing like what I expected a secondhand-shopping vegan to look like. She seems to have the cooking process under control. Bryce is in the back, washing dishes. Sweat drips from his forehead.

Meanwhile, Reza and Marcus are holding the bottom of a ladder while Marcus's aide, Rob, takes down the CoastFresh banner from above the serving counter.

"So . . . CoastFresh. Are they completely gone?" Simone asks Ms. Lydia, once we've dropped off our box of vegan condiments.

"Nope. Just taking it down because of new rules about corporate advertising. The school board's reviewing the whole sponsorship situation. I never liked those colors anyway," Ms. Lydia says.

"But you'll still serve their cheeseburgers," Simone says.

"We're celebrating our new vegan options, girl! Get with the program." Ms. Lydia's cheeks turn a concerning shade of purple. I tug Simone away.

"But there are still cheeseburgers, right?" Simone calls over her shoulder.

"What is wrong with you? I thought you were all about the vegan club!" I say.

"I am!" she insists. "But you know how people have meatless Mondays?"

"Okay . . ."

"Well, I was thinking I could have cheeseburger Mondays."

"I don't think you can be a part-time vegan," I tell her.

"This from the girl who eats pork curry in the bathroom." She rolls her eyes, but she's grinning at me.

Before I finish cringing at the memory, and before Simone and I can collect another box from the food truck, someone taps my shoulder.

"Richard!" I exclaim. "What are you doing here?"

"Ms. Lydia sent an email. After the lunch today, Amelie's mom is giving a cooking class for any interested parents. I thought I'd see what this whole vegan thing is about."

So maybe there won't be any more pork curry/bathroom emergencies. Without thinking about it, I throw my arms around Richard. It's sort of like hugging a barrel.

"Whoa," he says. "What's that for?"

"For making vegan lunches. And for coming to the climate march, too. And . . . well . . . I'm glad you're here."

The tops of his cheeks turn pink.

"Get the rest of those ingredients in here!" Ms. Lydia bellows.

Simone and I sprint for the truck, and Richard comes along to help. Soon, we have a whole table set up with napkins (biodegradable), condiments (vegan), soy cheese, lettuce, and buns. There are reusable cups for water, and not a CoastFresh logo in sight.

Amelie, Simone, Daniella, and I take our places behind the table. It's our job to keep everything neat and tidy. We've barely placed the last basket of apples when the bell rings. Reza and Marcus swing open the cafeteria doors, and people pour in.

Ms. Flores is one of the first in line, with Mr. Chadwick trailing behind her.

"Fabulous job, girls." She smiles. "What an amazing thing, to stand behind your convictions."

"I was simply trying to balance priorities," Mr. Chadwick mutters.

"Of course you were," she says. It doesn't exactly sound like she's agreeing.

When she stalks off toward a cafeteria table, he follows, still pleading. A minute later, I see her flag down Mr. Lau and invite him to sit.

"Amelie," I whisper. "Run a tempeh burger to Mr. Lau. Maybe he'll convert!"

She scurries off.

"Think there's a chance?" Simone asks.

I don't have time to answer because someone drips ketchup across our serving station. I quickly wipe it up and offer a clean bottle to the next student.

"Smells . . . not too bad," one of the boys says.

"It's not a cheeseburger," his friend mutters.

"Come back next week, for all-meat Monday," Simone says cheerfully.

"What?" Amelie asks, rejoining us.

"Pardon me?" I say, at the same time.

"That's not a thing," Daniella says, at normal human volume.

"Not yet," Simone says. "But don't discount the power of social media."

I pull out my phone. Sure enough, Simone has posted to YouHappy.

These tempeh burgers look terrifical. And they make me feel good about waiting until #AllMeatMonday for my next cheeseburger.

I can't help but laugh. And a burger of any sort sounds delicious right now.

"How long do we have to stand at this table? We get to try the tempeh burgers, right?"

As if I've conjured her, Amelie's mom arrives with four trays. She says she'll handle the condiment station for a while, so we load up with burgers, head to our usual spot in the cafeteria, and dig in.

"Not bad," I say.

Amelie beams at me.

Reza appears, balancing his tray in one hand while typing on his phone with the other. He slides in beside me. *Right* beside me.

Simone raises her eyebrows, but I glance past her as if nothing unusual is happening. Which is a little more difficult when my own phone buzzes.

> Climate documentary playing on Saturday.
> Want to go?

That was a text from Reza. Who is now oh-so-casually removing the pickles from his burger. But his foot's touching mine again.

> Okay.

Um . . . what? Did that just happen? Did I just say yes?

This is going to take some serious debriefing with Simone. And maybe with Amelie, because she seems like the kind of person who might know what to say on a date —

I will not be using that word.

While I'm busy trying not to look at Reza or Simone, my eyes land on Mr. Lau. He's still sitting with the other teachers. He has almost finished his burger.

Simone follows my gaze. "I heard that Asha offered to make another visit to Cedarview sometime soon. That should make him happy, right?"

Mr. Lau looks up at that moment. It's possible he gives me an infinitesimal nod.

My second bite of tempeh burger tastes nothing like cheeseburger, but it does taste a little like victory.

Students March for Climate Action
BY ETERNITY WILLIAMS

Organizers estimate that almost a thousand people turned out for Friday's climate march, the majority of them drawn by the need for immediate action on climate change. Others were drawn by the rumor of a surprise guest speaker: TV star Asha Jamil.

I caught up with Jamil before the march, along with her new friends, local youth activists.

"I'm so pleased to have this opportunity to help protect our environment and motivate young people to do the same," said Jamil.

And her efforts appear to be working.

"We've been huge fans forever," said eighth-grade student Emily Laurence. "And we're inspired by her commitment to climate action."

Laurence's friend, Simone Ahn, seemed just as excited about Jamil's poodle, a social media star in its own right. But Ahn was also enthusiastic about Jamil's commitment to the climate. "She's super-ifically inspiring," Ahn said.

"A role model," declared student Amelie Cattaneo.

According to a source within the school board, Jamil was originally slated to speak at Cedarview Middle School as part of a special event sponsored by CA Energy and CoastFresh. But students, teachers, and community groups — including local youth-led group The Climateers — sounded alarms about the increasing control that corporate sponsors are exerting over daily life within schools. The school board has promised to review its guidelines.

Climateers organizer Mya Parsons was thrilled to have Asha Jamil participate in the march.

"Celebrity engagement is amazing!" Parsons says. "But to address the climate emergency, we all need to take action."

With students like these in charge, I have no doubt the world is heading in the right direction.

AUTHOR'S NOTE

The Emily Post quotes in this book are drawn from *Etiquette In Society, In Business, In Politics, And At Home*, published in 1922. Because the copyright has expired, you can find the entire book online. More than a hundred years after it was written, it's still an entertaining read.

ACKNOWLEDGMENTS

People who at least pretend to think I'm funny: my mom, my sister, my best friend from high school, and — thankfully — Amy Tompkins and Lynne Missen. You are my dream agent and my dream editor, and I'm so honored to work with the two of you.

I'm also grateful for the amazing work of Bharti Bedi, Catherine Marjoribanks, Linda Pruessen, Indrid Alistair Bird, Graciela Colin, Daniella Zanchetta, Sam Devotta, Ericka Lugo, and Gigi Lau for helping bring this book to life.

My colleagues at the UBC School of Creative Writing are a constant source of inspiration and encouragement — thank you. And *Emily Posts* wouldn't exist without the Inkslingers: Rachelle Delaney, Kallie George, Sara Gillingham, Stacey Matson, Lori Sherritt-Fleming, Kay Weisman, and Holman Wang. Your ideas are brilliant and your etiquette flawless.

As always, a huge hug to Min for his endless support. And awkward side hugs to my children, Julia and Matthew, who refuse to give me any other kind.